D0631054

Fathers
&
Daughters

A Celebration
in Memoirs, Stories,
and Photographs

Edited by Jill Morgan

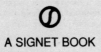

A SIGNET BOOK

SIGNET
Published by New American Library, a division of
Penguin Putnam Inc., 375 Hudson Street, New York, New York 10014, U.S.A.
Penguin Books Ltd, 27 Wrights Lane, London W8 5TZ, England
Penguin Books Australia Ltd, Ringwood, Victoria, Australia
Penguin Books Canada Ltd, 10 Alcorn Avenue, Toronto, Ontario,
Canada M4V 3B2
Penguin Books (N.Z.) Ltd, 182–190 Wairau Road, Auckland 10, New Zealand

Penguin Books Ltd, Registered Offices:
Harmondsworth, Middlesex, England

First published by Signet, an imprint of New American Library, a division of
Penguin Putnam Inc. Previously published in a Signet hardcover edition.

First Mass Market Printing, May 2000
10 9 8 7 6 5 4 3 2 1

Ⓟ REGISTERED TRADEMARK—MARCA REGISTRADA

Printed in the United States of America

PUBLISHER'S NOTE
Some of the selections in this book are works of fiction. Names, characters,
places, and incidents either are the product of the author's imagination or are
used fictitiously, and any resemblance to actual persons, living or dead,
business establishments, events, or locales is entirely coincidental.

CONTENTS

Contents

A FATHER'S LOVE:
AN INTRODUCTION
by Jill Morgan

I didn't have a good relationship with my father. Therefore, editing an anthology on the theme of fathers and daughters was somewhat of a challenge. It wasn't as if I didn't know what such a relationship should be, or even that I hadn't experienced it. Maybe not for myself, but I had seen it in others. Daughters who have lived without the benefit of strong, supportive fathers in their lives become keen observers of this in others, somewhat like a barren woman watching mothers with their babies.

From the moment I gave birth to a daughter, I witnessed the growing bond between my husband and our only girl. He was used to being a father to boys. Our two sons loved to be carried on Daddy's shoulders, or race around the house in mock terror while Daddy chased them with monster growls and appropriately gruesome faces. He was never too tired for this kind of horseplay. Most of the time he was as much a kid as the boys, and loved their rough-and-tumble games. I wondered if he would be a different sort of father to our daughter.

At first he was a little shy with her, as if this small pink bundle was too fragile, too different from what he knew and understood. Boys were easy, but a girl . . . that might be different. It wasn't long before his initial shyness ended, sometime around our daughter's first smile to him, or her babbled word "Da-da." After that he was charmed by her, totally and completely. The enchantment was permanent.

To our daughter, Daddy was someone who could fix any broken toy, be counted on to read stories to her in that wide, overstuffed chair, or talk Mommy into letting her stay up later than her bedtime to watch a funny movie on TV. He could build a three-story dollhouse (big enough for the cat to sleep in) or take the training wheels off a two-wheeler and teach her how to ride it, while running alongside to keep it upright. He was the one who taught her how to swim, holding his arms out to catch her as she jumped into the pool. She trusted him enough to know he'd keep her from drowning. He never gave her reason to lose that trust in him.

Being our youngest child, our daughter longed to be treated like one of her older brothers and not like the baby of the family. The nickname her father chose for her was Big Girl. He called her that long after she'd stopped hating being the youngest. I don't remember when he stopped calling her this, probably when her level of embarrassment rose higher than his level of enjoyment in continuing the childhood nickname.

Oh, how he hated seeing her grow up! "I wish I could put a brick on her head," he told me more than once. He wanted to keep his daughter little, still needing him, still adoring him, still sure he was capable of making everything all right.

Halloween was a favorite time for the two of them. He never missed it. For a man who never took a sick day from work, the fact that he took Halloween night off (he held down two jobs to support his family) was a big deal. He always seemed as excited as the children, helping them carve scary faces on the pumpkins. We had the biggest pumpkins on our block. Hang the expense. This was something important. He made sure he was home to help his daughter carve her pumpkin, and go trick or treating with her. It was a Daddy thing to do, and he never let her down.

For much of our daughter's childhood, her father was away at work. He would leave in the morning an hour before she awoke, and not come home until well after her bedtime. His long hours at two jobs provided good food for her, warm clothes, a nice place to live, and made sure she never wanted for anything. The only thing I'm sure she did want was seeing her father more often.

But there were special times. We attended a friend's wedding years ago, and I'll always carry the image of my four-year-old daughter and her father dancing a waltz, her small patent leather white shoes standing atop the toes of her father's dress black loafers.

As our daughter grew older, it was her father who took her to the store and helped her pick presents for me for Mother's Day, my birthday, and Christmas, teaching her that giving to others is a pleasure. He taught her to drive a car, fix a flat tire, file a tax form, and that voting in an election is both a responsibility and a privilege. The fact that she was a Democrat and he a Republican, and that they routinely canceled out each other's vote, didn't matter.

She told me recently of going to the library where her father worked nights, when she was about seventeen. He helped her find the books she needed for her school report, then walked her to her car, the way he always did, making sure she was safe. When she waved a casual good-bye to him, he threw her a kiss. That small act of tenderness touched her so deeply. Up until then she had thought her father did so much for her because he should, because that was his job and that was what fathers did. She realized at that moment he did everything because he loved her. He wasn't simply a man who went to work and paid the bills. He was a man who went to work and paid the bills because he loved his child. She decided then and there to make sure she spent more time with him, and that she wanted him to know how much she loved him, too.

One of the many ways she showed that love was through an anonymous gift of money, sent to her father's post office box, as a donation toward the restoration of his Mustang airplane. She let him think the money came from someone who had heard about his project to rebuild the old fighter plane, something he genuinely wanted. It was many years before he learned that the hundred dollars he was so surprised and pleased to receive came from his little girl, secretly giving her daddy a gift of love.

I watch them now, still observing this special bond between them, and note that these days it is our daughter who worries what her father will think of this new boyfriend, or that new job. She wants him to be proud of her—as if there were any way in the world that he would not be. When he and I debate some small issue and she sides with him, he jokes, "Thirty percent of my estate to Lisa."

The estate he has given her is worth far more than thirty percent. It is one hundred percent, total and complete, now and forever, the strong, supportive love of a father for his only daughter. No inheritance of any size will ever compare to that.

Within the pages of this anthology, in the stories written by celebrated women authors and their fathers, or in tribute to their fathers, the love shines through. Small as a little girl dancing on her father's shoes at a wedding, or great as a young woman sending a secret donation to her father toward the restoration of his beloved plane, the twelve offerings in this book are a gift to fathers and daughters everywhere.

Dear Daddy

Jill Morgan

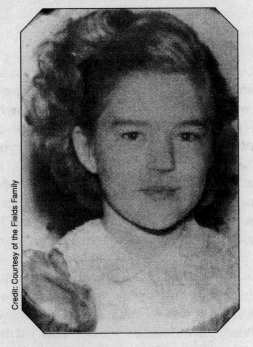

*Jill Morgan at eight years old,
the same age as the character of
Janey in this story.*

In the spring of 1944, American forces amassed units of fighting men in ships bound for the coast of France. Every ship held boys still in their teens, young men fresh out of universities, their first jobs, and farms. Beside these boys and young men sat sober-eyed husbands and fathers, men whose wives and children had been left behind. Among them, in one of the ships heading for the shores of Omaha Beach, was thirty-year-old John Casey. In Casey's hands was a letter from his only child, a daughter, eight-year-old Jane.

The sea pitched wildly, and men muttered prayers, asking God's protection from the waves, and for what was to come in the days ahead. Overhead, an unfamiliar trail of stars led them closer to a foreign shore, and to an appointment with Death . . . or Destiny.

April 20, 1944

Dear Daddy,

I'm sitting in my tree in the front yard writing this letter to you. I don't know where you are right now, but Mommy says you'll get my letter if I give it to the Army. I hope so. If you don't get it, write to me and let me know, okay?

It's nearly summer now. School will be out soon. I can't wait. I'm tired of school and books. I wish you were here so we could go on vacation to Jenny Lake in Montana. Remember when we did that? The lake was the best, and horseback riding! Mommy had to ride Old Blue. He moved in slow motion.

I've been asking Mommy to let me have a puppy for my birthday, but she says dogs are too much trouble. My dog won't be any trouble. I'll take care of him all by myself. When I get too lonely, missing you, I could hug him and I'd feel better. I'd rather have you back home, but until you come back, could I please have a puppy? I think if you told Mommy it's okay, she might let me have one.

When I start missing you too much, I write you a letter. It makes me stop crying. I don't let Mommy see me cry. But sometimes I see her cry when she reads your letters. When can you come home? In two weeks? Will you come home before

summer? We could go swimming in the pond behind Uncle Billy's house. I can swim lots better
now. Uncle Billy says I'm a fish.

I drew this picture of me so you won't forget
what I look like. I'm holding the puppy I want.
Isn't he cute? Will you ask Mommy to let me
have him? Please, please, please. He will keep
me safe until you get back. Sometimes I get
scared and I can't sleep. Mommy says I'm a wor-
rier, like you.

Come home soon, Daddy. I miss you.

Janey

April 30, 1944

Dear Janey,

Hi, Punkin. I loved your letter and put your
drawing right next to my heart. I carry it with me
everywhere. That's a pretty cute puppy. Looks
like a keeper. I'll put in a good word to Mommy
for you. Your letter sounds so grown-up. It makes
me realize how long I've been gone. I think you're
responsible enough to take care of a dog now, at
eight.

I'd love to be there with you this summer,
Smiley Eyes. Can't wait to see you swimming
like a fish. Keep practicing in Uncle Billy's pond.
When I come back, we'll go there together and

you can show me all you've learned. For a little while longer, I'll have to go where the Army sends me.

Don't think I'd ever forget your face, little girl. You and Mommy are right there on my eyes all the time. Be a good girl, Janey. Help take care of Mommy while I'm away. If you can remember, say a prayer for your daddy at night before you go to bed. I might have to be gone for a little longer than two weeks, Janey Girl. I may have to miss the whole summer. You know I'd be there with you if I could. There's nothing I'd like better.

Don't be scared, Janey. Your daddy's doing everything he can to keep you safe. Promise me something. Don't grow up too much while I'm away. You have my heart, Little Bit. Give Mommy a hug and kiss for me. And keep a special Always-Hug for yourself.

I love you this much (arms open wide).

Daddy

June 3, 1944

Dear Daddy,

You did it! I got to keep the puppy. Mommy read your letter and said you told her it was okay for me to have my dog. His name is Max and he's so cute. He rolls over on his back and wants me to scratch his tummy. He sleeps in my room at night, right beside my bed. Mommy said no about him sleeping in the house at first, but he whined so loud she gave in and let me keep him in my room. When Mommy's gone to sleep, I let him jump up to the foot of my bed. Don't tell Mommy I said that. She'll make him stay outside again, no matter how much he cries.

Mommy was going to make my costume for the school play, but she forgot to sew the buttons on. I had to pin it with safety pins, but I don't think anybody noticed. I tried to tell her about the buttons, but she was reading the newspaper and didn't hear me. When she stopped reading, I saw she had tears in her eyes. I didn't say anything about the buttons.

I'm glad I have Max, even if he isn't housebroken. You're a good, nice daddy for letting me have him. I drew you another picture of Max and me. He's the one with the long ears. Daddy, come home soon. I need to learn how to ride a two-wheeler, but I'm going to wait until you get back to teach me. Hurry, okay?

Grandma says I look like you, in my eyes. Sometimes I dream about you, and you talk to me. I'm so happy to see you, but when I wake up you're not here. Please tell the Army to let you come home.

I love you this much (arms stretching across the ocean).

Janey

June 5, 1944

Dear Janey,

This may be the last letter I'll be able to write for a while. The Army is sending us someplace to do a job for them. I can't tell you where I am, but I want you to know I'm thinking about you and your mother right now.

I'm glad you got your puppy. I won't squeal to Mommy about him sleeping on your bed. Max is a nice name. You're older now, Little Bit, and should be able to take good care of your pup by yourself. Mommy has lots of things on her mind, so try not to trouble her with puppy problems. I'll bet you can housebreak him if you keep at it.

Looking around me, I feel pretty fortunate. A lot of fellows over here don't have a family like I do. They sure don't have a sweet little girl like you at home, waiting for them. I know I'm one of the lucky ones. I want you to remember that, no matter what happens.

I love you more,

Daddy

June 8, 1944

Dear Daddy,

The newspaper says soldiers are fighting in Europe. Is that where you are? Mommy says you are with the men who landed at D-Day. Where is that? Daddy, can you swim in the ocean? I'm scared of the fish biting my toes in the ocean. Are you scared too? I can swim good now, but I can't swim across the ocean yet. Is it far?

School let out early, because of the war. Mommy says I have to stay at Grandma's house during the day so she can work at her new job at the aircraft factory. Grandma is teaching me to knit. When I learn how, I'm going to make you something. Don't guess what it is! You have to close your eyes and wait until it comes. Open your eyes if you can't see where you're going. I always swim with my eyes closed. Is that what you do in the ocean?

Mommy calls Max "that scamp" when he chews her shoes. He chewed a hole in my sock, but I wear it anyway. You don't have to keep it secret anymore about Max sleeping on my bed. Last night Mommy came into my room way after bedtime. I don't know what time it was, but she was dressed in her nightgown. She had your letter in her hand. I thought she was going to be mad about Max being asleep at the foot of my bed, but she didn't say anything about it. She just stayed in my room for a while, not saying anything. I pretended to be asleep. Then, right before she left, I heard her say, just like she was talking to you, "We'll be all right, John. I promise."

Grandma told me a story about when you were a little boy. She said you covered your ears on the Fourth of July when firecrackers went off. Grandpa says soldiers carry rifles. Are rifles as loud as firecrackers?

I do say a prayer for you every night, but now I say two, because you asked me special. I know God is listening. He keeps my daddy safe for me 'cause I cross my fingers when I pray, for extra luck.

I love you most,

Janey

June 9, 1944

Dear Janey,

We are resting after a long, hard day, and I found this scrap of paper to write a quick letter to you. I don't know if you got my last letter. I'm going to hope you did. I don't know if you'll ever get this one either, but I want to write it to you.

I feel very far away from home tonight. My comfort is thinking of you and your mother, safe and out of this nightmare. I will not tell you about this place. It's not a story fit for a little girl's ears. Believe this, sweet Jane, if there is any way I can come home to you, I will.

The stars at night are different here. Or maybe it's just me. I'm different. The whole world has changed. My sergeant has a little girl. Her name is Emily. He says she's eight, like you. If the world is made safer for little children like my Janey and his Emily, then what we're doing here will be worth it. I'm tired, Punkin. Too tired to lift my pencil a minute longer. God keep you safe from harm's way, Little Bit. I love you always,

Daddy

July 14, 1944

Dear Daddy,

Today was Grandma's birthday. We didn't have a cake. Mommy says we don't have enough rations for flour. When I'm big, I'm going to buy Grandma a pretty cake with yellow icing roses on it. Grandma says it's okay about not having a cake. She doesn't care. But I care for her. It isn't right.

Mommy works at the aircraft factory almost every day. She says if she does her best, maybe you will come home safe to us. What should I do to make you come home? Where are you, Daddy? Here's a drawing of me in our house. I'm looking out the window for you.

Please come home soon. I miss you.

Janey

P.S. Could you bring some flour when you come? Enough for a great big cake?

July 24, 1944

United States Army

Dear Mrs. Casey:

It is my sad duty to inform you that your husband, Lieutenant John Casey, is considered missing in action. His unit engaged the enemy on the field of France. With courage and honor, the brave men of this battalion fought to take a hill held by German forces. Under heavy machine-gun fire from the Germans, three men in an assault unit led by Captain David Williams took the hill and destroyed a machine-gun nest. Captain Williams and Private George Irwin lost their lives in the struggle. While your husband's body was not found, evidence suggests that he must have died with the other two men of this assault unit.

The United States owes such men as your husband, Lieutenant John Casey, a debt of thanks.

Please accept my sincere condolences for your loss.

> Lieutenant Colonel James Marker,
> United States Army

The two men who brought the telegram to her house were dressed in uniforms like the one Janey's daddy wore. She watched them through a small opening of her bedroom doorway. The air was hot, and the sun coming in the window behind her burned the patch of floor where Janey stood in her bare feet, so bad they nearly blistered. But she didn't move. She stayed and watched one of the two men take her mother by an arm and help her to a chair. The men spoke softly. Janey couldn't hear what they said. Her mother began rocking back and forth, holding the telegram to her heart. It was her mother's voice that Janey heard. No missing that sound.

Her mother cried out, "John! You can't be dead. You can't!"

And Janey closed the door.

August 1, 1944

Dear Daddy,

Last week two soldiers came to our house and gave Mommy a letter. The letter says you are lost. Don't you know the way home, Daddy? Remember when you taught me how to find my way to school? You showed me the big oak tree on the corner, and the blue house where I turn up the road. Just go back the way you came, and you'll remember.

I finished your present. It's a knit scarf you can wear in the snow. It was a surprise, but now I want you to know. Grandma tied all the knots so the stitches won't come loose. Don't you want to come home and see it? I wrapped it in tissue paper.

Grandma says I shouldn't keep writing letters to you. She says it makes me too sad. I don't feel sad when I write. I feel like I'm looking for you. If I was lost, you'd try to find me, wouldn't you? I'm going to keep writing. I'm going to tell you what we're doing, and maybe you'll remember how to turn back. Maybe you'll see the big tree on our corner and come home to us. Every night I ask God to bring you back to me. Daddy, come home. Don't be lost.

Janey

P.S. The telegram from the Army says you might be dead. But you're not. I know it.

August 7, 1944

Dear Daddy,

Mommy says we might have to give Max away. She says widows can't afford dogs who chew up shoes and aren't housebroken. Max is a good puppy. He doesn't know he's being bad. I try to teach him, but last night he chewed up one of Mommy's slippers. She swatted him with it, and he cried.

I went to Sunday school yesterday. The teacher told us a story about the prodigal son. He went away for a long, long time. He was lost from his family. He wanted to come home, but he was too scared. That story made me cry. Don't be scared, Daddy.

Uncle Bob comes over to our house and helps Mommy and me. He takes us shopping for groceries and cuts the grass in the yard. I like Uncle Bob. He's funny and sometimes he brings me candy. He gave me some dresses Debbie is too big to wear. I think they're ugly. They make me look like Debbie. Mommy says we have to make our money last. I'll wear the dresses even if they are ugly. When you see me, don't think I'm Debbie. Just look at my face and see it's really me.

When can you come see me? I made a wish on a star, but you didn't come home yet.

Come back right now!

Janey

August 14, 1944

Dear Daddy,

Grandpa gave me a flashlight to keep next to my bed, for when I have bad dreams. He says I shouldn't bother Mommy at night. She comes home from work at the aircraft factory, too tired to talk. She falls asleep before I do. Grandpa says I have to be a grown-up girl.

Tonight, I had the worst scary dream. I dreamed I saw you, someplace far away. I called you, but you didn't hear. I ran, but I couldn't catch up. You kept walking, like you didn't see me. And then you were lost. I couldn't find you. It was so dark. I woke up and turned on my flashlight.

I'm under my covers, writing this letter. Daddy, you have to be some place where you can't see me, or hear me, or you would write back. If you are lost, follow my letters and come home. I don't want to be a grown-up girl, like Grandpa says. I want to be your little girl again.

Please come back. I miss you.

Janey

August 29, 1944

Dear Daddy,

Today, I went into your room. Mommy was at work. Grandma had to stay late at the dentist. I was alone. I was looking for you, because you're lost. I found your watch. I wound it up and put it on my wrist. It ticked. I put on your coat, the leather one, and sat in your chair. I put my feet in your shoes. I closed my eyes and you were here.

I don't let Mommy see me cry. I don't let Grandma know I still write to you. I don't tell Grandpa the batteries burned out in the flashlight. I just wait. When will you come home? I drew a picture of our house. Do you remember? Can you still see me on your eyes? Can you see Mommy?

Max doesn't chew our shoes anymore. He's housebroken, most of the time. He digs in the yard. One time he dug up Mommy's flowers. She was mad. But he doesn't chew shoes. He's a good dog.

I'm waiting for you. I look out the window for you every night. In the morning I go to your room to see if you are there. I know you want to come home. Mommy says you would come home to us if you could. She says maybe you were hurt too bad and had to go away.

I took your watch to my room. At night I'm going to hold it in my hand and hear it tick.

I love you this much, Daddy (arms open wide).

Janey

The patient in the bed at the end of ward three had no name. He was a soldier, still in an American Army uniform when found, but so badly injured by the grenade blast that nearly took his life, even his military dog tags were beyond recognition. In the front-line triage unit that first assessed his injuries, the wounded were divided into three categories: serious, critical, and dying. The soldier was left to die. Hours later, when he stubbornly remained alive, he was flown by Army transport to a small English country house turned convalescent hospital, in Arundel, along the Southdowns coast. For weeks his condition showed little improvement. He slowly regained consciousness and gradually regained enough strength to be fed by the nurses, but the concussion he had suffered during battle left his mind closed to any memories of the past, including his own identity.

In early September 1944, another soldier arrived at the convalescent hospital in Arundel. His name was Lieutenant Mike Stevens. His right leg was shattered beyond use, but his mind was clear. His eyes had been burned by the same explosion that destroyed his leg, and were heavily bandaged to protect them from light as they healed. Mike Stevens was given the bed next to the patient at the end of the ward, the man the nurses called John Doe.

For two weeks, while doctors waited for Mike Stevens's eyes to heal, Stevens spoke in a one-sided conversation to the patient in the bed beside his, never discussing the war that brought them both to this place. John Doe remained silent. When Stevens asked, the nurses said only that the other patient was so badly injured, he wasn't expected to live.

On a chill September night, the evening before the bandages on his eyes would come off, raw fear claimed Stevens. He wept, unable to control his terror. On that night John Doe spoke to him, becoming Stevens's eyes and describing the sweep of fall across the English coast. John Doe filled in the colors that Mike could not see, told him about the other patients in the ward, and lent him a calm courage as Mike waited to learn if he would be blind as well as crippled. But for John Doe there was no one to fill in his blind spaces. At the edges of his mind were fragments of images he couldn't quite grasp. It was as if the grenade that exploded, causing his injuries, had broken his life into shards too fragile and sharp to piece together again.

In the morning, when doctors removed the bandages from Lieutenant Stevens's damaged eyes, the caring nurses of Arundel House waited breathlessly to know what Stevens would say. He was a favorite among them, young, handsome, and friendly. Stevens turned toward the patient in the bed next to his own, opened his eyes, blinking several times.

"Can you see?" asked the doctor.

It was to the amazement of everyone in the ward when Stevens answered the doctor's question with the words, "My God, it's John Casey!"

September 10, 1944

Dear Daddy,

I made this drawing for you. See me? I'm holding my flashlight that Grandpa gave me. I got new batteries. I'm standing by my tree with the swing you made. Remember how you pushed me way high? Remember when I fell that time, and Mommy said I could have cracked my coconut?

See the sunflowers in the front yard? Grandpa helped me plant them again this year. Some of them are bigger than me! The birds eat the seeds.

Grandma is teaching me to cook. I can make deviled eggs. When you come home, I will make you some. Grandpa says he likes my deviled eggs better than Grandma's, but I think not really. He wants to teach me how to ride my two-wheeler, but I told him I'm waiting for you. Grandpa says I'm like you, stubborn.

Do you want to know a secret? I think you're following me home, but only when I dream. Every time you get a little closer. I can almost catch you, but then I wake up. Do you see me when you dream? Daddy, close your eyes.

I love you more,

Janey

September 14, 1944

On a windy afternoon, just before sunset, a telegram arrived at the Casey home, delivered by a young messenger on a bicycle. The leaves had begun to drop from the liquid amber trees in the yard, creating a carpet of autumn colors. The boy, no more than fifteen, trod the leaves underfoot as he crossed the yard and climbed the two wooden steps to the front porch. He rang the bell, setting off a volley of sharp barks from Max.

Janey sat in her tree, watching, unseen by the young messenger at the door. Hidden, she saw it all from high on the branch of the tree. Saw her mother open the front door. Saw the look that crossed her mother's face. Saw the hand that took the telegram and opened it with trembling fingers. Saw her mother sit down hard on the wooden floor of the porch. Without a chair. And heard her mother cry.

United States Army
September 14, 1944

Dear Mrs. Casey:

It is with utmost pleasure that I inform you that your husband, Lieutenant John Casey, has been located and that his name has been removed from the Army's list of missing in action. Lieutenant Casey is presently at a convalescent hospital in the Southdowns of England, recovering from serious injuries sustained in battle.

Another patient at the convalescent hospital, Lieutenant Michael Stevens, recognized Lieutenant Casey, having known him while in the same infantry unit. Lieutenant Stevens immediately wrote a letter to his commanding officer, describing in detail the events which led to Lieutenant Casey's heroic actions of taking a German machine-gun nest after both of his companions on the assault team were killed. Not only was

Lieutenant Casey successful in accomplishing his mission, which saved the lives of countless American soldiers, but he also prevented German forces from controlling the road to Calais, a road which is crucial to Allied forces.

For his heroism on the field of battle, Lieutenant Casey has been awarded a Silver Star, the nation's second-highest military honor, plus a promotion in rank, from Lieutenant to Major, effective immediately, and the thanks of a grateful nation for his courage under fire. For injuries received in action, your husband will receive two Purple Hearts.

Although your husband has not yet made a full recovery, his doctors in Arundel, England, assure me that he is receiving the best medical treatment for his very serious wounds. I join with you in prayer for the restoration of his health, and his rapid return to the United States, and the loving arms of his family.

> With my sincere best wishes,
> Lieutenant Colonel James Marker,
> United States Army

A packet of letters that had been held by the Army for Lieutenant John Casey, missing in action, arrived at Arundel House Convalescent Hospital. The handwriting on the envelope of each letter was in a childish script, large and written in pencil.

Brought to the bed of the patient at the end of the ward, the letters remained unopened and ignored. For two days John Doe, whose bedside chart now identified him as Major John Casey, made no effort to read or even touch the mail. Nurses suspected his near-fatal head injuries might have caused too much damage to his mind. A discussion took place among the staff, suggesting sending Major Casey stateside to a long-term care veterans' facility. The visible wounds to his body were healing, but there were doors to his mind that seemed irreversibly closed.

That would have been the final course for Major John Casey's life had not a simple request from Lieutenant Stevens, because he had no mail of his own to read, changed everything.

"Lieutenant, I mean, Major Casey . . . are you planning on reading those letters?"

"No."

"Because if you're not, I was wondering if it might be all right if I looked at one or two of them?"

"Yes."

"I guess that must sound peculiar," Stevens went on, failing to register that Casey had spoken.

"Yes."

"It's just such a *big* stack of letters," said Stevens. "You see, I haven't had any mail in a long time."

"Yes."

"I could kind of pretend. Wait . . . what did you say?"

Major Casey pushed the bundle of letters toward Stevens, saying nothing more.

"Really? All of them?" asked Stevens, gingerly reaching for the whole pile. "Well, all right!"

Stevens eagerly sorted them, putting them in order by postmark. "Looks like they're all from the same person."

Stevens found the one with the oldest date. "Guess I'll start with this one. Sure you don't mind?"

Casey didn't respond.

Stevens was careful not to spoil the writing on the envelope as he slipped his penknife under the flap and sliced it open along the envelope's fold at the top. "Let's see, now. What do we got here?" he said, pulling out the letter. He sat back on his bed, plumped his pillow, stretched out and got comfortable, and started reading to himself.

Dear Daddy

The words stopped him. He cut a glance at Casey, uncertain how to proceed. Somehow, he hadn't thought the letters could be from Casey's kid. It didn't seem right now. No one but Casey should be reading these. Letters from a girlfriend, or even a wife . . . he might have done it. But not letters from the guy's kid. That was just plain wrong.

"You should probably read this yourself," Stevens said, holding the letter out to Casey.

Casey kept staring at the wall, as if seeing some far distant battlefield, or the place where his mind lingered.

"Okay," Stevens said, "then I'll read it to you."

He began, "Dear Daddy . . ."

As Lieutenant Stevens read the simple words written by eight-year-old Janey Casey, something as apparent and trusting as the love of a child for her father stepped across a barrier and opened the locked doors of John Casey's mind, where hidden memories of war had held him captive.

Casey's first reaction was a ragged indrawn breath, like a dying man struggling for air. Lieutenant Stevens heard this. Encouraged, he kept reading the letters, one after another. When he read Janey's words, *Don't you know the way home, Daddy?* Stevens looked over at Casey and saw tears glistening on the man's cheeks. He stopped reading, suddenly afraid that he had done the wrong thing. That he had made things worse.

"Go on," said a voice.

Lieutenant Stevens turned and was surprised to see the ward doctor standing behind him. Stevens hadn't known the man was there, or that two ward nurses were listening as well.

"Keep reading," said the doctor. "That child, she's doing what all our medicines couldn't do for him. For God's sake, keep reading."

Stevens saw the faces of other patients in their beds along the ward. Wounded men, with injuries that might claim their lives, were turned toward him and listening. In each of their faces Stevens saw the light of hope kindled in their eyes, a remembered love, to light the way to family and home.

Stevens kept reading. *I found your watch . . . I put on your coat. . . . Can you still see me on your eyes?*

A sob broke from the soldier courageous enough to take on an enemy machine-gun nest all on his own, when every other man of his battalion had died in the struggle. John Casey came back from the war that night. Wounded, and scarred. Exhausted, and shaky with the realization that he had survived when so many others hadn't. Good men. Sons, husbands, fathers.

In a voice that threatened to break with his own emotions, Stevens read Janey's words from the last of her letters. *Do you want to know a secret? I think you're following me home, but only when I dream. Do you see me when you dream? Daddy, close your eyes.*

The road home for Major John Casey, for Lieutenant Michael Stevens, and for all the injured men of Arundel House Convalescent Hospital's ward, was drawn by the simple landmarks of a child's world, and printed in the healing words of a daughter's love.

October 13, 1944

On a day unlike any other, when the sky looked swept by streaks of color, pale gray, magenta, and a thin wash of pink, Janey sat in the crook of her tree and waited. A breeze lifted fallen leaves from their pillowy drifts covering the grass. The air tingled with expectation, and a change of light brought the moment into sharp focus, as if becoming suddenly clear.

Janey leaned forward, sensing : . . knowing. Something was different.

Far in the distance, a tall, blurred shape began to emerge from the shadows. She watched, hope racing in her heart. Stared with eyes that had seen this same familiar image far away before. Someone walking, coming nearer. Slowly, the color of khaki becoming the image of a man. A soldier.

The man stopped, as if seeing her, too. He lifted his hand in a wave, and shouted something she couldn't hear. Then Janey was down from the tree and running . . . Max barking wildly behind her, and the words she had waited so long to say forming on her lips.

"Daddy . . . you're home!"

AFTERWORD

Elements of this story are true. My father did serve in the infantry. He did land at Omaha Beach on D-Day. With an officer and another soldier, he did take a hill held by the enemy and destroy a German machine-gun nest that had pinned down Allied forces. He was awarded a Bronze Star for valor, not the Silver Star mentioned in this story. He did receive two Purple Hearts for injuries he sustained in action, and other medals for remarkable achievement, exceptional courage, and proficiency in the skills of battle. He did spend time in a convalescent hospital recovering from his wounds. This much is fact.

In my childhood I did sit in a special tree in our yard, imagining a world far away from my own. Unlike the character of Janey in this story, I was not born until after the war was over, being one of the first children of the baby boom generation. As a young girl, I knew very little about my father's experiences during World War II. We never discussed them until I was an adult. Even then my father was reluctant to recall the memories of that time in his life. I have taken liberties with the bits and pieces I have heard from him, and created characters that are mostly fictional, but shaded with truth.

Part One

Coming of Age

The Summer of
My Womanhood

Faye Kellerman

*A bonneted Faye Kellerman
at the age of four months
with her perplexed father.*

M y father wasn't a distant figure in my child-hood, but I certainly didn't know him well. Like many men of the World War II generation, he worked excruciating long and hard hours, not for career fulfillment or self-enlightenment, but in order to pay the mortgage on a Veterans Affairs–financed three-bedroom, one-bath house in the hot, dusty San Fernando Valley of Los Angeles County. My father was in the retail food business, not by default but by choice. His decision, especially since he came from a religious Jewish background where education had always been prized, always puzzled me.

When World War II broke out, Dad was drafted. Instead of immediately being sent to Europe, he was deemed smart enough by the army to send to college. After two years of attending classes at Rutgers University, studying subjects that obviously excited him—he spoke about them well into my young adulthood—he was offered officers training. Declining the chance for advancement because it meant a longer tour of duty, he was shipped overseas and into the infantry. God must have shined His light on Dad because he spent only two weeks in the front lines, though it probably felt like years. After the brief stint he was reassigned to the medical corps. Trained as a medic, he desperately tried to save what the enemy was determined to destroy. After the war Dad's fluency in Yiddish made him invaluable to the army because he understood many of the languages spoken by concentration camp victims. He would often translate for his superior officers, aiding in placement and relocation of those who'd survived the Nazis' final solution.

When he talked about the war, it was not often and not very much. But I do remember what he told me. Yes, he revealed stories of the human atrocities, but he was much more intrigued by the ability of ordinary people to rationalize those horrors away, of the denials in Polish towns where the stink of the crematoriums could be ascertained for miles. It affected his lifelong outlook. How could it not.

Honorably discharged from the army, my father did what most newly married men did back then: they took jobs not for their glamorous titles but because they needed money. Even though Dad had passed entrance exams to local law schools, he decided to skip three years without income in favor of immediate cash. My father became Oscar the Deli Man—following in the footsteps of his father—Judah (Edward) the butcher.

I'm sure money had much to do with it. But after observing my father at work up until he died, I do think he was happy with his occupation. It was back-breaking toil, which involved, but wasn't limited to, toting hundreds of pounds of meat, lifting cases of canned goods, shivering in walk-in freezers and coolers during the winter in stores with no heat, and putting in ungodly hours—from dark to dark. Sunlight was something that glared through plate-glass windows. But the money he earned was from the sweat of his own brow, and that was good enough for Oscar Marder.

As a small child, I was often put to bed before Dad came home. As an older child, I remember watching TV with him. He didn't talk much except to ask me if I had yet guessed the plot of the latest *Streets of San Francisco* or, at the very least, the quarterly subtitles given after each commercial break during the hour show. Heart-to-hearts were nonexistent, but some sort of primordial communication—that of father and young daughter—did exist.

Dad staked out his claim by renting space in independent food markets. Usually he ran just one operation at a time. Occasionally he managed two locations. His booth consisted of a fresh delicatessen with all the traditional meats, cheeses, salads and, of course, lox and pickled herring. He also took on a small bakery that catered and complemented items sold in a deli. His breads included loaves of soft yellow egg challah, carraway ryes, savory onion rolls, kaiser twists covered with poppy seeds, and oh, those aromatic fruit and cheese Danishes and coffee cakes. Dad's kiosk had everything needed for the perfect Saturday picnic or the in-law Sunday brunch. I loved the food, and I loved everything that went along with it. Because I loved my father.

When my older brothers reached double-digit age, they worked in the deli on weekends and helped my father out. When I was eleven, no such demands were made of me. This, of course, angered me. If Dad wasn't going to require it of me, I'd simply require it of myself.

When I announced that I was going to work at the deli, Dad said that was fine, although I was sure it wasn't fine at all. But that didn't stop me.

He didn't know what to do with me. Being

short and slight, I didn't fit the job description. There was a physical component to the work that called for muscle mass. I had none. The most skillful chores required an adeptness with sharp objects—meat slicers, cheese slicers, knives for trimming and cutting lox. I had small hands and fingers—way too little to handle industrial equipment that could slice a digit as easily as a corned beef.

Of course, there was the retail side—the greeting and the waiting on customers. I was too short to be seen above the countertops. To the consumers on the other side, I was more or less a floating head. My father was constantly dodging me because I was underfoot and the operating space behind the counters was minimal. The starched white apron my father gave me for protection was way too big. It dragged on the baseboards, picking up sawdust around the hemline. Occasionally I'd trip on it. When that happened, I hiked up the cloth. Eventually it would fall down again.

I'm sure I was a disaster. I'm sure I got in Dad's way. But he never said anything to me about it.

Dad knew I couldn't remain an ornament. He had to give me something to do. My first assignment was shoveling the three most popular salads—potato, cole slaw, and macaroni (this was prior to the urban elite *pasta* salad)—from the cooler into pint or half-pint containers. This job was a snap because the salads were priced by the pint. A pint of cole slaw was x amount of cents. A half-pint totaled x/2. I was a math whiz in school. I had absolutely no trouble figuring out how to halve things.

Having mastered salads, I was given my next assignment—the weighing and wrapping of dill pickles. This, to my surprise, turned out to be a very tricky affair.

I was given a stool in order to see and read the scale. But first I needed to learn *how* to read a scale. Back then, before the advent of LCD and the digital revolution, watches were analogs and scales were mean critters consisting of columns of prices and rows of weights—a veritable crisscross of numbers that bounced up and down with a spring weight. To find out how much something cost necessitated finding the correct intersection between price and weight along a skinny red line. I've known adults who never mastered the art of reading this kind of scale, just as I've known those who never got the hang of a slide rule.

It took me some time. For the first week all my pickle prices magically came out in pounds, half pounds, or quarter pounds because—being a math whiz—I could divide the price by factors of two. Anything in between was rounded off to the nearest whole number divisible by two. In order to please the customer, I usually rounded down. I'm sure I cost my father some pocket change.

If he noticed it, he never said anything.

Eventually I vanquished the scale. It was a proud moment that should have been worthy of some kind of certification. But knowledge has its own rewards. Reading the scale now allowed me to *weigh* things—items like lox and precut cheeses and meats, fishy pickled herring and the wonderfully oily Greek olives.

With two skills mastered, I was determined to crack another—wrapping. Origami enthusiasts needn't have worried. Still, I was proud of my neatly swaddled packages with just the right amount of sticky tape on them. And when I wrote the word "pickles" or "Swiss" on the white paper in my own handwriting, no one could have been more pleased than I was.

My weighing and packaging skills had been honed to such an extent that Dad took an enormous chance. No, I was still forbidden to use the meat slicers, but he let me try the bread slicers.

For those unschooled in the literature on bread slicers, I shall explain. To slice a whole loaf of bread, one usually places the bread against a back bar, then turns on the machine. With a manual handle—which the operator slowly pulls toward him or her—the bread is advanced and forced between a series of moving parallel blades until it emerges out the other side in neat, perfect slices.

Immediately upon exiting the blades, my first rye fell apart, the slices fanning out like a deck of cards. Spotting the trouble, Dad once again explained to me that as the bread advances between the blades, it is necessary to secure the loaf on the other side with your hands. This must be done with care as fingers are not supposed to get close to the blades. Was I up to the challenge?

Indeed I was. After a couple of failures, I was finally able to produce a successfully sliced loaf of rye. I was even able to hold it aloft, vertically by the heel, as the experts did.

Alas, it was the next step that tripped me up. I placed the rye *directly* into the white wax-paper bag. Needless to say, again the rye fell apart.

As I apologized profusely, the customers just laughed it off.

Isn't she cute?

C'mon, guys. I'm trying to do a job here.

Of course, the crucial error was not housing the rye in a tight plastic bag and securing it with a flexible steel tie before I placed the loaf into the white wax-paper bag. Of course, that step necessitated opening the plastic bag while still holding the rye in the air.

Not an easy task of coordination. A few of my loaves ended up as fodder for the sawdust floor.

More waste.

If it bothered Dad, he never said so.

Eventually I snagged the coordination necessary for packing the ryes. And not just ryes, loaves of challah and wheat bread as well. These were a challenge unto themselves because challahs and wheat breads are much softer. They required a *delicate* touch with the bread slicer.

Not one to rest on my laurels, I demanded more. Dad must have felt that I was up to the ultimate challenge because he put the entire bakery under my charge.

The entire bakery and I was only eleven.

This was monumental.

Faye, the bakery lady.

Pick a number, please!

There I was, wearing a hair net, slicing breads, twirling plastic bags with a flourish, and handing out free sprinkle cookies to toddlers.

The coup de grace came when Dad started taking me to the wholesale bakery to pick out items for our little bakery. Of course, we chose the usual rolls and breads and bagels and Danishes. But now, since Dad had a genuine bakery lady, he began to invest in more coffee cakes, coffee rings, *bobkas*, and cookies.

The smells were incredible. Hot and yeasty doughs laden with sugar, chocolate, nuts, and cinnamon, glazed with thin white frostings. The aromas, more than the visuals, made my mouth water. We chose our fare straight from the ovens, still hot, resting on parchment paper. At first my dad made all the selections. As I got bolder, I began to make a few suggestions of my own. Sometimes he listened. Sometimes he did not.

One week there was a particular coffee-ring cake that appealed to my eye as well as to my nose. It was a typical yeast, cinnamon dough topped with circles of cherries, lemon, blueberries, and apple, the fruit swimming in seas of pectin and sugar. I had to have it. Though not particularly aromatic, it appealed to my eye.

"It will never sell," Dad said.

"But it's pretty."

"People buy with their noses, not with their eyes."

"People like fruit rings," I countered. "And if it doesn't sell, we can take it home."

I was the youngest in my family, and the only daughter. I batted my eyelashes and Dad melted. Arriving at the store before the opening hour, I set out the coffee cakes, the cookies, the rolls, and the breads. I tidied up the plastic and paper bags. Unplugging the cord to the bread slicer, I cleaned it of yesterday's crumbs and seeds. I plugged in the bread slicer. Then, with my duties done, I waited for the customers to come out of the starting gate.

Our first consumer came in a few minutes after the doors opened at nine. She was a forty-plus woman—Jewish as many of our customers were—who scrutinized my baked goods. I saw her eyeing my pretty coffee ring. The artificially red cherries, the egg yolk–colored lemon filling, the blueberries, and the apples.

She scrunched up her brow. "I'll take that one," she stated.

My father was looking over his shoulder as I scooped the cake under my hand and placed it into a pink bakery box. Tying it with bakery string.

"Bingo, skittle ball in the old pocket," he whispered to me.

I had never heard the expression before. And Dad never used it again. But I never forgot it.

I decided to take on the job full-time during my summer vacation. It was hard work. I was on my feet most of the time, and I worked four- to eight-hour shifts. Halfway through the month of July, I experienced an epiphany. I was not going to do this for the rest of my life, putting up with cranky customers, flaky vendors, the whims of mechanical equipment, and fallen arches. I made a decision to go for an advanced educational degree. Though writing wasn't in my sights at the time— I never had the audacity to dream I could get published—I was still a person with many options. I could be anything I wanted to be. What I wanted more than anything was to do interesting work while *seated*.

One morning right after the store opened, I went to the rest room and realized, after a very startled reaction, that I had begun menses. Enormously embarrassed, I didn't know what to do. Sneaking off, I called my mother from a pay phone, and she came to pick me up. No stickem pads back then. We girls were inducted into the clumsy world of belts and napkins. After the problem had been secured, Mom took me back to work.

She must have said something to my dad. He came up to me with a perplexed look on his face.

"Are you okay?" he asked with the concern of those men who stayed clear of *female* things.

"I'm fine, Dad."

"You're sure?"

"Positive."

"I think you have a customer."

"Then I'd better go help her."

After that moment there were no more references to female things. We were just two people trying to earn an honest buck.

Wilding

—∞∞∞—

Mary Willis Walker

*Mary Willis Walker and Ralph Willis
in the tribal rite of celebration after
Mary won the Edgar Award for
Best First Novel of 1995.*

Credit: Ezio Petersen

FOREWORD

When I was eleven years old, I had an encounter with fear which revealed to me that there are far scarier things in heaven and earth than the monsters and bogeymen I had previously dreamed of. I was playing at a construction site in our neighborhood with a friend when we got carried away—the term *wilding* comes to mind—and lapsed into an orgy of destruction.

That night I had the mother of all nightmares. I woke consumed with terror, frightened nearly out of my mind. I was certain I had committed an irrevocable crime, and that my life was over because of it.

Weeping, I woke my father and poured out the whole story. When he fixed it, made everything all right, relief poured over my body like warm, healing water; I felt reprieved, cleansed, newly-born. All my previous anxieties seemed insignificant. It was a genuine, real-life catharsis.

What I aspire to as a writer of crime fiction is to re-create that kind of emotion in my reader. It's unforgivable hubris to say that, I know, but since the very act of writing fiction requires enormous arrogance, I figure I might as well go for broke with my aspirations. I want to seize the reader by the throat and shake her up with the worst kind of nightmare, the kind that springs from her own violent impulses. We all have those impulses. In the throes of adolescent fervor, we have committed reckless pranks that could easily have turned deadly. Exhausted at three a.m., we have wanted to throw a colicky, squalling infant out the window. And in the middle of an angry divorce, it has occurred to us that it would be easier—and more satisfying—just to kill him. Crime stories appeal to us partly because we need to read about people who have actually acted on these same impulses that flit moth-like against the screen doors of our minds.

But presenting the nightmare, arousing the fear, is only the first part of the job. What is more difficult is orchestrating the finale, the catharsis, which delivers to the reader that intense rush of pleasure that follows the cessation of fear. I want to leave her breathless with relief, her innocence restored, her anxieties calmed.

So where is it, this miraculous, emotional roller coaster of a book? Well, I haven't written it yet; my skills aren't up to the task. Nonetheless, I continue to dream of doing it.

The best writers of our genre do manage to do it: they dredge up our own evil, terrify us with its bloody consequences, and then, God-like, they deliver us from that evil.

WILDING

Standing there on the hard gray concrete slab with her eyes narrowed against the morning sun, Stella, who never thought much about the future, was struck with a glimpse of it: the field was going to be spoiled. For all her eleven years, this field, across the street from her house, had been hers, the place for catching grasshoppers in mason jars, the place where you could disappear into the long, dry summer grasses that whirred and clicked with hot insect noise. The narrow dirt path through the field was her shortcut to the swimming pool, a shortcut that often ambushed her with offerings—fragments of a sky blue egg, a tiny skeleton, or, at the end of the path under an arch of vines, a steamy pile of dog turds alive with glossy, iridescent horse flies.

All that would be ruined now. A new house was already rising up from this gray rectangle, its wood frame invading the space. It would grow substantial and neat and perfect, and all around it smooth green grass would roll out, like brand-new wall-to-wall carpeting you were forbidden to walk on. It would cover the field, smother it, kill it.

She braced her navy blue Ked against a copper pipe sticking straight up from the concrete and was surprised to feel it bend slightly. "They aren't working today," she said to her friend Carol, who stood down on the ground surveying the deserted construction site.

"Labor Day or something," Carol muttered through pale hair that fell forward like lace curtains, blurring her profile.

Stella pressed the pipe harder with her foot and slowly it gave way, surprisingly compliant. "Think I can do it?" she asked.

Carol shrugged, standing there in her tight white jeans, looking bored and distant. Ever since she had started getting her period a few months ago, she had stopped being fun, and Stella missed her.

Now the pipe was bent far enough so that

Stella could rest her foot on top and put all her weight into it. She asked again: "Think I can?"

Carol didn't answer.

"I think I can, I think I can," Stella said, mimicking the chugging rhythm of the little engine that could, trying to get Carol to laugh. She stood on the bent pipe, threw her arms out to balance herself, and forced it all the way down to the concrete. "Wooo-ee!" She stepped off and looked down at her handiwork. The pipe was bent to a right angle and nearly broken off at the base.

Stella leaned down and grabbed hold of it, trying to rip it free, but it hung on stubbornly. She twisted and pulled, feeling her arm muscles lengthen as she strained. Suddenly the pipe snapped off. Surprised, she stepped back and held it out, showing it to Carol, whose eyes glittered now with interest. Stella took the pipe back over her shoulder the way her father had taught her to throw a baseball—like a boy—and with all her might she hurled the pipe into the sky. They watched it fly, spinning end over end, rose-burnished in the sunlight; it arced and dropped into the tall grass of the field.

Carol stepped up onto the foundation, finally, and wandered around until a plastic bucket full of nails caught her attention. The sun was getting hotter, and the grasshopper hum around them was getting louder, like the whine of high-voltage wire. Carol hoisted the heavy bucket with both hands. "Think I can?" she asked, with her old wicked smile, as she upended the bucket, spilling the nails out onto the cement. She threw the empty bucket into the field and scattered the nails with her foot. "I thought I could."

Stella let out an involuntary snort of delight, ran to the next pipe, and pushed it with her foot until it bent under the pressure. "I think I can, I think I can," she chanted, feeling her excitement rise. She forced the pipe to an angle where she could stand on it. This time, as it sank down toward the concrete, she lost her balance and had to run forward to keep from falling. She caught herself by grabbing the wood frame of what looked like a doorway. Under the impact of her weight, it shook. She laughed, surprised to see how flimsy it was. She felt powerful, as though she could shake the whole house down, like Samson pulling the temple down, or the big bad wolf huffing and puffing. "I think I can!" she shouted, shaking the frame deliberately this time. Carol took hold of the other side, and together they rocked it back and forth, gently at first, then harder and faster. "I think we can!" Stella chanted, "I think we can!" The door frame tore from its moorings with a ripping sound. With one mighty last push the girls sent it toppling to the slab.

Carol threw her head back and laughed the way she used to before she got braces and the curse—her mouth wide open and her face scrunched up, making a wild donkey bray. Her face was red and wet with sweat now, like a hot tomato about to burst in the sun. She picked up a bucket of scraps and whirled it around, then let go and watched it fly out into the field.

Stella moved from pipe to pipe, systematically breaking each one off. Together the two girls shoved a stack of boards and some wire coils off the foundation. In a frenzy now, they used the broken pipes to pry up boards; they tore down as much of the framing as they could; they dumped the contents of every bucket, every box. When they were finished, their chests were heaving and their shirts were drenched with sweat.

Stella picked up one of the pipes. It was jagged at the broken-off end and warm to the touch. She laid it against her cheek and looked up at the sun overhead, gazing directly into it. People always said not to do that, you could go blind, but Stella didn't believe it, she did it all the time. She liked the way it broke the world up into dazzling, wild kaleidoscopes of color. Still staring at the sun, she stretched her arms out to the side as if in a trance and began to spin. She knew without looking that Carol was spinning too—their old game, their old intoxication. Stella accelerated, spinning faster and faster. The object of the game was to do it until you were completely dizzy, then to stop suddenly and not fall.

After a few minutes, Carol squealed, "Let's stoooooop!" Stella did, and she felt the foundation rock and lurch under her feet. It tilted, rose up, and smacked her hard. From where she was sitting, she looked around and saw Carol staggering like a drunk sailor, laughing hysterically, strands of blond hair stuck to her wet face.

But Stella was not laughing: she'd seen the rivulet of blood snaking down her leg where she'd cut herself with the jagged edge of the pipe when she fell. The cut was just above her knee and barely hurt at all, but the blood was bright and disturbing. She pulled a wadded-up Kleenex from the pocket of her shorts and pressed it to the cut to stanch the flow.

She couldn't go home because her parents would want to know what happened and she could never tell them. So the two girls took the path to the swimming pool. They begged Band-Aids from the life guard and used the bathhouse to wash and bandage Stella's cut. The rest of the day they spent sitting at the side of the pool, talking, but never mentioning what they'd done at the construction site.

When Stella got home that night, she couldn't remember ever having been so tired. She was too tired to eat dinner, too tired to play baseball with her father the way they usually did after dinner. She said she might be getting sick, she'd better go right to bed. When they asked about the bandage on her leg, she said she'd cut it on a bottle at the pool. It was nothing.

Stella dreamed that the house across the street did get built, exactly as she had foreseen the morning she stood on the foundation. It rose up relentlessly, each day more closed in and perfect and solid, until it loomed over the field—a white two-story brick colonial with a three-car garage and walled terrace. And just as she'd foreseen, one day the green lawn was rolled out and the field was gone.

The new family moved in—two parents, two babies, three children who might have been around her age, some big dogs, and an old granny. The night after they moved in, Stella woke in the middle of the night with a tight knot of fear in her chest. Silently she slipped out of bed and went outside, barefoot, in her pajamas. The night was very dark with no moon or stars, but she could see perfectly:

the new house, bright white in the darkness, was trembling and shaking on its foundation. As she watched, the slate roof and the chimney crumbled and collapsed, the brick walls heaved and crashed in. In total silence it collapsed on top of the sleeping family inside—the babies and the parents and the dogs and the kids her age and the old granny. When it was over, nothing remained but flat, dusty rubble, like a bombed-out village in a war movie.

Stella stood there studying the devastation she had made. She knew exactly what had happened. The house had collapsed because they hadn't noticed the damage to the foundation, the damage she had done. They just went ahead and built the house, and now it had collapsed. She had killed this whole family. It was done and nothing could change it. Her life was over.

Stella woke quaking, drenched in sweat, her heart pumping wildly, her stomach convulsing. In terror she jumped out of bed and ran to her parents' room.

She stopped at the door and looked in at her sleeping parents—so peaceful and innocent—and she envied them. She would never sleep like that again. She tiptoed to her father's bed and touched his arm. "Daddy, Daddy." He woke quickly and took her hand. "Stella. Baby, what is it?"

She sat down on the edge of the bed, and the story gushed out of her—the damage they'd done at the construction site and the horrible thing that had just happened.

"Such a bad dream," he said.

"No," Stella said. "It really happened. The house fell on them and crushed them all."

He swung his legs out of bed and stood up. "Let's go see." He led the way to a window that looked out across the street to the field. He stood aside for Stella to look. A crescent moon gave just enough light for her to see the large gray, rectangular slab of the foundation in the middle of the field. No rubble, no collapsed house. No dead babies. It was miraculous, as if time had reversed itself to give her a second chance.

When her father came back the next morning from his discussion with the builder, Stella was sitting on the doorstep waiting for him. "Did you show him everything, Daddy?" she asked. "The pipes? The wood? Everything?"

He nodded. "He's going to fix it all and send me a bill."

Stella shut her eyes. A few huge, hot tears of pure joy leaked out from under her closed lids.

Her father leaned down and put his arms around her, kissed her on the cheek. "It's over, honey. Forget it." He straightened up and went into the house.

Stella turned her face up to the sun, feeling its warmth as if for the first time. She wanted to open her eyes wide to it, to invite it to transform the sky into an explosion of dazzling starbursts, but she couldn't make her eyes open; the lids were too heavy and the light was far too bright for her.

AFTERWORD
by Ralph E. Willis

Mary's recollection of this incident is essentially correct, but she was not—and still is not—aware of how this was settled.

I was in the final stages of resolving a lawsuit in which our neighbor-to-be and I had been involved for several months. Both parties to the potential settlement were on hair-trigger terms, and an incident such as Mary had engaged in just might tip the shaky prospects of adjudicating a sensible settlement.

To involve two little girls in such a matter seemed pointless. I consulted an old friend, an architect, who knew the contractor and was willing to go to him and arrange for a fast repair job over that weekend. The owner, fortunately, was away for that entire week, so, to my knowledge, he never knew what had happened. There was, of course, no cost to him, and the acid test was satisfied that no future problems could result from the damage.

I told none of this to Mary or her friend. I don't want to sound too heroic here: my objectives were to avoid causing trouble for the girls and to avoid upsetting the resolution of my legal matter.

Over the years that passed after the event, the two girls were high-spirited, but not on the wild side. The act itself never seemed to me one that deserved punishment beyond the guilt they imposed on themselves. The memory of the unhappy little girl who woke me in the middle of the night is one I recall frequently, a constant reminder of my love for her.

Mary's comment:

I really *didn't* know that. Is there a family alive that has no secrets? I think not.

Gifts of Love

Maxine O'Callaghan

A. B. Parrish in Tennessee,
1943.

Maxine O'Callaghan
today in California.

While standing on a forklift and greasing the overhead cranes in a plant that made cold-drawn steel, my dad slipped and fell twenty-five feet onto a cement floor. He died about five hours later—a hard death that ended a hard life.

He was born John Griffin Parrish in a small town near Birmingham, Alabama. For some reason my grandfather was away at the time, maybe looking for work that would take him out of the coal mines. When my grandmother died in childbirth, a barren aunt sent him the message that the baby had died, too, claimed my dad for her own, and changed his name. She called him A.B., just the initials, which, as far as I know, didn't stand for anything. This was the name he always used. A few years later, when my grandfather returned and discovered his sister-in-law's deception, he took his son from the woman my dad loved dearly and always thought of as his mother, and my father was raised by that stern, cold man and his indifferent second wife.

Dad lived in grinding poverty in both homes, only finished first grade, could neither read nor write. As soon as he was strong enough to do a day's work, my grandfather took him along to the mines. I think my dad was twelve. He escaped that dreary fate because my grandfather developed black lung disease and took up an itinerant ministry.

Eventually, they wandered into western Tennessee, where Dad met my mother. He was nineteen when they got married; she was fourteen. They had ten children, only to lose five of them, four at birth, one as an infant of two months to pneumonia.

During the Depression he picked cotton and strawberries, shoveled out barns, dug ditches for the WPA. A move to the southeastern corner of Missouri just after World War II improved our family's hardscrabble existence slightly. It wasn't until my brothers and I were old enough to provide a decent labor pool that Dad became a sharecropper. This step up in the world came late, however, just when cotton farming was becoming mechanized. And so a few years later he moved on to that foundry in suburban Chicago where he died.

He was sixty-two years old.

*   *   *

These are the facts of my father's life. Like all statistics, they tell you nothing of the person who is reduced to cruel numbers and impartial dates. Memory alone provides glimpses of the living, breathing human being with all his faults and virtues, and even these bits and snippets are filtered, colored, imperfect. Still, they are all that is left and all that I can offer in remembrance.

The summer I was fourteen, a girl at school told me my dad looked like Humphrey Bogart. It startled me to realize she was right, that he had the same lean, lantern-jawed look, the same quizzical squint as he lit a cigarette and stared at you through the smoke. Years of outdoor manual labor kept him pared down to hard, corded muscle. Beneath the overalls and long-sleeved shirts his skin was white as marble, but exposure to the sun had tanned his arms and face a leathery brown and cracked the skin on his neck.

My dad, the summer I was fourteen. Of all the memories, good and bad, this is the time and place I want to remember.

The rest of America was busy making up the good old days of the fifties, those middle-class myths of carefree childhood and a future where all things were possible. Nothing in my family's life remotely resembled this Ozzie-and-Harriet world, but things *had* taken a turn for the better, and it seemed that they just might keep on improving.

After years of day labor, Dad had talked the manager of one of the larger farms into letting him have ten acres to raise cotton on shares and a house that seemed like a mansion by comparison to the mean little shacks we'd been calling home. In retrospect, I think the farm manager must've lived there at one time before he built the modern spread about a mile down the road. The place had only four rooms, but these were large with lots of windows. Several big old trees provided blessed shade, one of them an enormous willow that trailed feathery branches over a wide front porch.

There was a barn and an entire row of out-buildings all linked together, including a hen house that retained a potent smell of dung and which our chickens refused to inhabit. They preferred the barn, and, frankly, I didn't blame them.

One of the buildings, some kind of old shed, was in such a state of disrepair, Dad tore it down, leaving only a few posts in the ground. To these he attached chicken wire to form sides and a roof and planted morning glories. By August the vines covered the wire in a dense green canopy. This cool, leafy retreat was mine, off limits to my two younger brothers and little sister, and they knew better than to test our father's edict. He called it my playhouse, although I was too old for one, had never had one in any case.

Since I was the oldest of the surviving children, and a girl to boot, I had taken on adult responsibilities very early. At eight, when my mother went to work in the fields, she left me in charge of my brothers and a wood-burning stove. Today this would bring Child Protective Services running. Back then these things were necessary if we were to eat and have clothes on our backs. I'm sure that playhouse was my father's way of making up for the loss of so much of my childhood.

For furniture he found an old table and two spindly chairs, nailed together some planks from the shed debris to make a couple of benches, and added a roof beam to support a porch swing. I would do my homework at the table, bring a pillow and curl up in the swing with a book whenever I could sneak away. I loved the place and filled it with odds and ends I'd collected: old iron tools and horse tack I'd found out in the barn, mason jars full of dried weeds, lard buckets filled with dirt and planted with moss roses and alyssum.

I'd like to think I realized what a special place

that playhouse was, what a special time that summer was in our lives. It's too sad to think otherwise, because by the next spring it would all be gone. On the first day of spring, to be precise, the twenty-first of March. Dad rarely kept us home from school, but that day he did, to help plant the quarter acre of garden out behind the barn. All afternoon the clouds moved in from the west, the hair stood up on our arms from static electricity building in the air, and that night a series of tornadoes dropped out of the sky. We were trapped in the house with the roof caving in and the walls coming apart, listening to that terrible freight-train roar as the twisters demolished the barn and my playhouse along with the other outbuildings, ripped up the trees, and destroyed everything we owned, leaving us with only our lives.

But in this memory it's still summer, a particular morning in late August, and if things did not happen exactly as I relate them here, if I've compressed time and added details, I make no apology. I'm a storyteller, after all, and my father's child.

One thing for sure, it was already hot in the kitchen, and heat shimmered outside in the cotton fields that surrounded the house. At seven o'clock my dad would have been up for hours.

He arose every day at four a.m., a lark in a nestful of surly owls because we kids took after my mother, who always looked stunned and haggard until noon.

One gloomy winter morning he had tried to explain the appeal of rising early to me, saying, "Oh, sugar, no matter how bad things are, no matter how bad they've been, that ole sun comes up, I get the feelin' today's the day something real good just might happen."

When I said, "Daddy, it's cloudy. It's dark outside. It's *raining*," he only laughed.

"Well, ole Sol's still up there, ain't he?" he'd said. "Just 'cause you can't see him don't mean he ain't up there, shinin' behind the clouds."

That morning he was happy as usual, cheerfully ignoring my mother's scowls. While he poured fresh milk into a big glass jar, he began telling us in relentless detail about everything he'd done since he climbed out of bed.

Understand, when my father told you something, you didn't just listen, you relived the entire incident with him. He said, "I got to the garden right after breakfast. Good thing, too. I keep telling you boys you can't let that johnsongrass get a foothold. Sneaky stuff, johnsongrass, but it wudn't no match for me, not first thing this morning." He put the milk in the icebox, and went to pour himself some coffee. "Big dewfall, my pant legs got all wet, but I didn't care 'cause it was so nice and cool, and the dew was all beaded up on the leaves with the sun shinin' on it. Looked like it oughta be set in a ring, pretty enough for some rich lady's finger."

He rambled on as he poured Country Gentlemen tobacco from a cloth pouch onto a cigarette paper, expertly rolled a smoke, and fired it up as he took us from the garden into the barn with the sun streaming through the cracks and dancing on dust motes and the cow stamping around, impatient and complaining about her swollen udder. I swear when you listened to Dad's description you could feel that old cow's teats in your hands and smell the fresh, creamy milk splashing in the pail.

At breakfast, however, nobody in our house appreciated these wonderful details, except for three-year-old Debbie, whose circadian rhythms hadn't changed yet to match ours. My brothers, eight and eleven, hunched over their eggs and biscuits, not even ready for their ongoing contest to see who could deliver the hardest kick under the table and not get caught. As for Mom, she was seven months pregnant with her ninth child and just wanted the meal over with so she could go sit down and complete the process of waking up.

Dad never held it against us, but he never shut up, either. He kept on talking as he stood by the table smoking, drinking his coffee, and waiting for me to finish breakfast. All the while he never took off the battered felt hat he usually wore.

"Come on, sugar," he said, stubbing out his cigarette as soon as I swallowed the last biscuit crumb. "Something you have to see."

He led me outside to the playhouse, refusing to answer my whiny "What is it, Dad? I have to get ready for school. I don't have time—"

Dragging me along, he ducked inside the viny cave, pushed his hat back, and stood looking up. "Ain't that the most beautiful sight you ever saw?"

Overhead, the morning glories were open. The sun shone through the silky blossoms so that they seemed to vibrate with a pure blue light. All I could do was stare, my breath caught in my throat.

Dad said softly, "It's like little pieces of the sky fell down and got stuck in the leaves."

We stood there silently for a few more seconds. I said, "Thank you, Daddy," or at least I hope I did, before we went back to the house.

Inside, Mom was off in a bedroom arguing with the boys about misplaced homework. Dad's bellow brought them scrambling and hurrying out with the screen door banging behind them.

"Wait up," I yelled, picking up my books, pausing to say, "Dad, you are coming to school?"

"They givin' you a hard time again?" he asked.

"Oh, you know . . ." The staff in the superintendent's office was sure to harass me if my father failed to show up for his part-time job, but I never told him how much their badgering embarrassed me. "As long as you're there today, it'll be okay."

"Well, I told Mr. Jones I was going and I am," he said, although both of us knew that if the man who ran the farm had decided a field needed plowing or an errand couldn't wait, there was not a thing Dad could do but comply.

My father's determination that his children have an education was not the norm for families like ours. His resolve baffled Mr. Jones and irritated him as well, so he seemed to go out of his way to make it difficult for Dad to work a few hours a week at school.

"Don't you worry," he said, going off to say good-bye to my mother.

My little sister came racing out of the bedroom as he went in. She bounced up and down, red curls flying, blue eyes wide with urgency as she said, "I wanna play in your house today, Mackie. Tell Mommy I can do it. She'll listen to you. Please, please tell her."

"Baby, you know I can't do that," I said.

Losing four children had turned my timid mother into a fearful person. Her fears bordered on paranoia during this pregnancy, afraid not only for the baby but that something would happen to Debbie. When the two were there alone, she wouldn't leave the house, and she wouldn't let my little sister out of her sight.

I said, "Be a good girl and don't give Mommy any trouble. When I get home, you and me will go out there together, okay?"

This got me a reluctant nod and then a hug so fierce I had to pry her chubby arms away from my waist while the boys shouted for me to hurry or we'd miss the bus.

I went to catch up with them. The district provided no bus service on dirt roads, so we went one way, a half mile to the county blacktop for a long, roundabout ride, while Dad went the other. We had no car, so he'd walk about a mile to make an obligatory stop at the manager's house and then, depending mostly on the man's mood and generosity, he'd walk another mile and a half to school.

My father was not a perfect man. Although he never raised a hand to me, he'd often take a switch or a belt to my rambunctious brothers.

He was a different person then, reverting, I believe, to the dour, unforgiving father who had raised him. I'd seen my grandfather only rarely, but I remember being afraid of him. In the few photographs I have of him, he looks like some Old Testament patriarch, always dressed in black and holding a Bible.

Although I'm sure he tried, this stern old man never broke my dad's spirit. Dad might have been uneducated, but he could talk to anybody, anytime, on any subject. With an easy smile and his Alabama drawl, he'd talk about the St. Louis Cardinals, the price of cotton, how Reel Foot Lake was formed when the earth shook and split open and the Mississippi River flowed backward to fill it.

I grew up thinking that last one was just a tall tale until I read about the great New Madrid earthquake in 1811, the Really Big One that still hasn't been topped by California or Alaska. You'd think something so momentous would have been taught in school, but local history was not a part of our curriculum.

Years later, I was to learn that this land along the Mississippi was a rift valley where ancient floods had deposited fifteen hundred feet of topsoil, about a hundred times more than in Iowa. This fertile earth produced dense forests and was home to deer and panther and bear. While the river helped create the bounty, that broad, muddy water also brought destruction by providing an easy shipping route. And so the animals were hunted down and driven out, the huge oaks, sweet gums, and cypress clean-cut and sent north to make everything from houses to egg crates.

This particular area in the Bootheel of Missouri was swampy as well, so once the trees were gone, the government built a network of drainage ditches that allowed the rich loam to be farmed. Look at a map and you'll understand why that southeastern corner of the state was called the Bootheel. It actually lies below the Mason-Dixon line, something I was never proud of, but most people were. When I lived there, the land was flat and nearly treeless, with the dusty green of cotton rows broken only here and there by a few fields of corn and soy beans.

I've learned you need mountains and ocean to provide some scale so you get a feel for size. Without them that place seemed small and somehow claustrophobic under a blue dome of sky that trapped the heat and humidity.

Now, you can tell people you were raised on a farm, but they still want the name of the closest town. I usually say Steele or Caruthersville, not that these are places anybody would recognize, but because people laugh when I tell them I grew up near Cooter, Missouri.

With a population of about five hundred inhabitants, the term one-horse town or wide spot in the road is a perfect description for Cooter, which was not named for a bird or a hicky old guy, but for a turtle that was one of those species exterminated by the loggers, engineers, and farmers.

The three-story red-brick school that housed Consolidated District No. 5 was by far the largest building in town, and the district was, I'll bet, the biggest employer. From here buses gathered kids in grades one through twelve from all over Pemiscot County.

After a break during May and June, the school year began in July, with another break in early September. This schedule accommodated cultivating and harvesting the cotton crops. During those hot summer months the classrooms were small and stifling; in winter they were stuffy and overheated. Teachers enforced strict discipline with big wooden paddles, and the books were mostly defaced and outdated. Still, I loved the place, and I loved my father for his dogged efforts to keep me there even when the cotton crop wasn't quite in sync with the school breaks.

Unlike Dad, lots of parents weren't willing to give up the income their children provided, so schooling came out second to money. Compulsory education? Well, yes, through fifth grade, as I recall, and, I presume, there were truancy laws. Economics ruled, however, so none of this was enforced, and the attrition showed in the layout of that old three-story building.

First and second grades, two classes of each, shared the bottom floor; third, fourth, and fifth were housed on the second. The rest, grades six through twelve, occupied the third, with enough room for a library and the principal's office.

When the bus arrived at school that day, I was fairly sure Dad wouldn't be there yet, but I tracked down the full-time janitor anyway.

He just shook his head. "A.B.? Nope, ain't seen him."

There was nothing I could do but go along to the administration offices, busy on Monday morning with kids coming in to pick up weekly cafeteria tickets or to drop off written excuses for absences. The office was the only place in the building with air conditioning, kept cold enough so I'd be shivering before I left. I think there were venetian blinds and, maybe, green carpeting. The only details I vividly recall are the high counter, like the kind you find in doctors' reception areas, with a desk on the other side, and the big, round clock on the wall behind the counter.

Strange what you remember about people and situations. Years later I attended a high school reunion for which most of the town turned out. I didn't recognize the friendly woman I eventually identified as the administrative secretary who had sat behind that high counter, but she certainly remembered me, and with what seemed like genuine fondness. Even after that meeting I can't fix a face or a name in my mind. What's very clear is the memory of the dread that knotted my stomach every week when I had to confront her.

It's not easy to look down your nose at somebody when you have to look *up* at them, but somehow that woman managed the trick.

"Yes?" she snapped. "What is it?"

"I'd like lunch tickets for my brothers and me," I said.

She made a show of taking a blue-covered account book from her desk and opening it, although we both knew what the columnar pages would show.

"Your daddy hasn't been here in two weeks," she said.

"He's coming today," I said. "Or tomorrow at the latest."

"Well, just wait over there a minute," she said, indicating with an irritated wave a spot at the end of the counter. "We're going to have to talk about this."

I stood there with my cheeks flaming while she laughed and chatted with the other kids who went in and out. The routine took place every week, and there wasn't a one of them who didn't know why I was left standing and waiting.

Education was compulsory, but this did not mean it was free. The district charged a book fee, and some supplies were required. Not a lot, but then it was a critical amount with three kids who couldn't attend school shirtless and barefoot. So my dad had gone to the superintendent with a plan. He went several times, as I recall, before he talked the man into it. Dad would do janitorial work at the school, but he would receive no money. Instead, what he earned, which was far less than minimum wage, would be credited toward the book fees and toward a hot meal in the cafeteria every day for the three of us.

This worked fine except when Dad had no surplus hours to draw on. Even though he'd been working there for two years, had never failed to put in the time he owed, the school only grudgingly extended credit, and I was the one who had to ask for it.

I had a terrible feeling that this time I'd have to go talk to the superintendent. This had happened one time before and was an ordeal I didn't care to repeat, but with every tick of the big, round clock, I became more certain Dad was not coming.

Then, suddenly, he was pushing through the door, looking hot and dusty from the country road, sweat making a wet band around his hat and trickling down his temples. Squaring his shoulders and tilting his hat back, he smiled his Bogart smile and began telling the woman what a pretty day it was, how the maypops and honeysuckle were all in bloom down by the drainage channel, asking her about her children and her mother, saying how sorry he was about taking so long coming in to work and what fine, fine people they were to trust him and take care of his kids.

She didn't want to be charmed and cajoled, but she was, and five minutes later I left with three lunch tickets and a brief hug from my father, who whispered that a day which started out so beautiful just naturally had to end up that way—and he would have a surprise later on to prove it.

My dad was an only child, but my mom had seven living brothers and sisters, and they in turn had lots of kids. Out of all of them, thanks to Dad's determination and hard work, I was the first ever to finish high school. Still, even though they had little education, the women in Mom's family loved to read.

Most of my relatives, including my grandmother, had moved over from Tennessee to the Missouri Bootheel. A born-again fundamentalist who spoke in tongues, my grandmother read only the Bible, but Mom, her sisters, and her nieces passed around any reading material they could get their hands on because there was little money for such luxuries. Their favorites were true-confession magazines and paperbacks with lurid covers, but anything would do. I learned to read the same way, voraciously and indiscriminately.

For me the school library was a treasure trove. By that summer, when I was a freshman in high school, I'd had access to the library for more than three years. First I'd skimmed off the cream: Hugo, Dickens, Brontë, Shakespeare; then I simply started at one end of the shelves and read my way through to the other, A to Z. Mom read some of these, too, but she was pickier than I was and much preferred *Forever Amber* to *Jane Eyre*.

Although my father was illiterate, he loved a good story, especially a western, and I often read to him. His one extravagance was a magazine called *Texas Rangers*. Evenings he would sit, listening intently, smoking and losing himself in the exploits of those hard-riding, sharp-shooting lawmen.

Volunteering to work in the library during my study hall gave me first crack at any new books, but nothing had come in all summer. I was down to rereading a few science fiction novels, which I was able to hold on to because none of the others in our family network liked the genre.

Walking home from the bus that afternoon, I expected it would be awhile before I had time for reading or anything else, and I was right. My mother had spent the day shut up in the house in the merciless heat with my little sister, too enervated to do more than rinse and stack the dishes and make the two of them a skimpy lunch. She looked pale and haunted, her ankles so badly swollen the bones had vanished in the puffy, bruised flesh. Debbie's skin had broken out in a heat rash, and she was wild to be outside. Mom let her go reluctantly, then went to sit on the shady front porch with her feet up so she could keep watch.

I could hear her out there as I cleaned up the kitchen, yelling at Debbie to stay where she could see her, screaming threats at my brothers if they let anything happen to her. Trying to cheer her up, I told her about Dad's promise of a surprise, but she was in no mood to entertain a happy thought.

"He sure can't buy nothin'," she said, "unless he's been hidin' some money. It's probably just some silly thing he found at the dump."

She finally fell asleep on the porch, only to wake up hungry and out of sorts and wanting to start dinner even though Dad always came home late when he worked at school. After we ate, I saved a plate of food for my dad and cleaned up the kitchen again. Then I finally kept my promise to Debbie and took her out to the playhouse.

The sun hung on the horizon, molten orange, shimmering in the still, moisture-laden air. Out in the fields not a leaf stirred on the waist-high cotton. The intense heat had started popping the fat green bolls like popcorn. The rows would be ready to pick in a couple of weeks, probably just before school was out. I can still remember the smell of that ripening field, a powerful odor, dusty and slightly astringent. The scent of cotton fabric doesn't even come close.

It was much cooler in the playhouse. The morning glories were tightly curled, so there was just the dense green of the leaves overhead. Still plenty of light, but it had a serene, underwater quality.

I sat in the swing and did algebra while Debbie chattered away and served her doll cookies and tea. The boys had gone to take care of the cow and, I suspected, to play in the barn loft.

I wonder now if my life might have been different if that storm the following spring had passed us by, if we'd continued to prosper. When you live in a nice house in a nice setting—even if nice is a relative term—it's easier to compromise, to settle for something less than ideal. Who knows what might have been?

But the tornadoes did come boiling down, and after endless days of living as refugees in an uncle's overcrowded home, we moved into a small cinder-block house with walls so porous that rain would seep in and run down the unsealed blocks, with one scrawny tree outside and a tiny front yard of dirt so barren nothing would grow in it, not even weeds.

Losing clothes and furniture is one thing. What we lost was far more fundamental and critical: our confidence in simple acts of hard work and faith in the future. The experience also underlined for me just how clearly the caste lines were drawn, because nobody offered help except those who had little to give. So it was mostly relatives who pitched in with only enough of the basics so we could eke out a marginal existence.

Although I loved my family, I came to hate that dreary house, the ugly landscape, and the unrelenting poverty with such an abiding hatred that all I wanted to do was escape.

I stuck it out until high school graduation, and within the week I was gone. With ten dollars and a bus ticket and a ride to the bus stop in Holland, I'd leave while my father was off working in the fields because I knew if I had to say good-bye to him, I wouldn't be able to go.

But on that August day when I was fourteen, I was content in the moment. I'd probably finished my homework and was writing something—a poem, a science fiction story to be destroyed in the tornadoes, and no great loss.

Debbie heard Dad before I did, whistling to let us know he was coming. She cried, "Daddy!" and charged out of the playhouse to run and meet him. I went after her. He was silhouetted against the sunset, and I could see he was carrying a big cardboard box up on one shoulder.

My sister danced around him as he walked through the yard and up to the porch where Mom was sitting. "What is it, Daddy? What did you bring us? Is it for me?"

"Oh, be quiet," Mom said, but I could see she was intrigued in spite of herself.

Dad put the box on the porch at her feet and opened it. "This here's for you, baby," he said to Debbie, and took out a coloring book. Most of the pictures had been filled in, but she would find a few that weren't and she would be happy just to turn the pages and add her scribbles.

"The rest is for you two," Dad said.

Images on the slick covers were bright even in the twilight. *Saturday Evening Post, Redbook, Colliers', Ladies' Home Journal.* Three or four months of each magazine, all of them thick with fiction because this was before the *National Enquirer* and *Vanity Fair,* before *Hard Copy* and the *Jerry Springer Show,* before content took second place to advertising.

"I saw this great big stack sittin' by the back door at Mr. Jones's house this morning," Dad said, "ready to go in the trash. I asked if I could take 'em."

"Oh, Mom," I said. "Isn't this wonderful?"

"Wonderful," she repeated with a look on her face that some women get when they receive gifts of fine jewelry and long-stemmed roses.

"I told him we'd sure like to have some more, too," Dad said. "If they could just put them magazines in a box for me, then I'd pick 'em up and bring 'em home."

And that's what he did, for a long time afterward, one of the few things that made life bearable in that awful new house we would live in.

People change. Life changes them, not always for the better. After I left home, my family moved to the suburbs of Chicago. There my dad would do menial, repetitive work in an environment without color and light, and live in a place that was as alien as a foreign land. So my brothers and sisters—Debbie and the little girl who was born in October the year I was fourteen—remember a different man, valid memories and not to be discounted, but so are mine.

I remember my father's gifts to me of unconditional love, his pride and his belief that I was a special person, his sacrifices that ensured I would have a better life. I remember that he had the narrative skill of a great storyteller and the eye of a poet. I remember that he taught me that a person needs to dream even when those dreams seem impossible.

Within a year after my dad died, I published my first short story. A few years later, the first of my novels was in print. My greatest regret is that he never held one of my books in his hands, and I never had a chance to say, "Thanks, Dad, I couldn't have done it without you."

My Father the Communist

⟨⟩⟨⟩⟨⟩

Eileen Goudge

Credit: Courtesy of the Goudge Family

*Eileen Goudge, age one, holding the hand
of her father, Robert James Goudge.*

In memory of my father
Robert James Goudge
1923–1998

In 1961, the year I turned thirteen, a quiet revolution took place in our cul-de-sac. Like weeds in a sidewalk, it seemed to spring out of nowhere, slyly and without warning—turning coffee klatches into war councils, and making enemies of friends who'd car-pooled and baby-sat each other's kids and even vacationed together. Common ground for neighborhood barbeques and after-hours highballs became fields for reconnaisance missions that had my friends and I sneaking under the cover of night with our flashlights into the very backyards in which, over the years, we'd consumed vast quantities of hot dogs and Kool-Aid on splintery picnic tables, and chased each other around inflatable Doughboys.

The opening shot was fired by the Cruikshanks next door. Early one Saturday morning an earthmover appeared out of the blue and began tearing up their backyard. Myrna Littleton rushed across the street to confer with my mother. Parked at our kitchen table in her housecoat, puffing furiously on a Chesterfield, she sniffed, "I should have seen it coming. Bobbie Cruikshank always has to be first. Last week, that two-for-one sale at Gemco's? I don't have to tell you who was in line right in front of me. Now look at her—the first one with a swimming pool."

But the hole wasn't wide enough to be a swimming pool. "They must be digging up the old cess tank," speculated my father, rattling his newspaper for emphasis. "You know what that means, don't you? We'll be doing the same before long."

He was referring to the fact that all the houses in our subdivision had been built the same year—just after the war, when babies had taken the place of munitions as our country's gross national product. My sister Libby was three, and according to family lore my mother "big as a house" with me, when, after months of looking at models and spec homes, my parents settled on Hacienda Acres. It was Mom who'd cast the deciding vote. In an era when every street in America was named after a tree, here each one was named after a different bird. We lived on Cardinal Place, a sleepy dead end where to the best of my knowledge no cardinal had ever been spotted.

It turned out that Myrna and my father were both wrong. By mid-afternoon it became apparent that something even more insidious was afoot. With my best friend and I practically falling over each other to see out my upstairs bedroom window, the hole next door began to take shape. Not, as Suse had darkly predicted, a secret tunnel that would connect the Cruikshanks' house with ours and allow fat Herbie Cruikshank access to the mini-fridge in our den. Nor was it, as Libby surmised, like the prim little adult she'd become, underground storage for the booze Mr. Cruikshank was rumored to drink too much of.

It wasn't long before we learned the truth, from snot-faced Herbie (who else?). In a lofty tone made laughable by his adenoidal whuffling, he informed us, "When the commies drop the bomb, you'll all be creamed tuna on toast while me and my folks are playing Scrabble in our bomb shelter."

Herbie couldn't have known it, but his superior attitude, an echo of his parents', no doubt, was the call to arms, so to speak, for the Cold War soon to divide our neighborhood.

By the start of summer, six other families had begun construction on bomb shelters of their own.

Each night over supper, the merits of various air-filtration and water-supply systems were discussed, sometimes heatedly. If Mr. Smith was putting in four hundred square feet, Mr. Jones next door would draw up plans for *five* hundred—and throw in a flush toilet as well. Suse's father made his position known one evening at the dinner table by intoning with grave authority, "With the Bomb, there's no such thing as playing it too safe." When Suse argued against it, saying there wouldn't be enough room left in their yard to flip a burger, and if the stupid Russians wanted to bomb us they should just hurry up and get it over with, she was scolded sharply, and I was sent home.

But Suse was that way, always thinking in the short term. Like when we had been getting ready for our eighth-grade dance and she turned the iron on high to make it heat up faster. She'd had to tie a sash around her waist to hide the scorch mark on her dress, which hadn't seemed to bother her one bit. It just wasn't her nature to think the worst. Take Khrushchev, for instance. Where I saw a scary bald guy with his finger on the button, Suse saw someone robbing her of a patio and barbeque pit.

So, yes, I understood about Suse. It was my father's reaction that shocked me to the core. Dad was the smartest man I knew. He taught world history at the high school in Placaville, and had been a pilot in the air force during the war. He smoked a pipe in an age when everyone else smoked cigarettes, and was the only one on our street who had the *L.A. Times* delivered every morning along with the *Placaville Courier.* When I approached him in a panic, demanding to know why *we* weren't protecting ourselves against a nuclear blast, if he even *cared* that we'd all end up creamed tuna on toast, Dad gave me this long look and said simply, "I'm not afraid of the Bomb, Lisa. It's *people* that scare me."

He wasn't the only one who refused to go along. Mr. Clarkson, three doors down, put his foot down as well—the only one he had left. He'd lost a leg in the war, and had a steel plate in his skull that according to Mom had left him a little funny in the head. So when he ranted that if the commies got any "big ideas" they'd have to get past him first, no one took him too seriously.

There were a few other holdouts as well, but they kept a lower profile. You'd see them scurrying past a house that'd been taken over by dump trucks and men in hard hats, their eyes averted in shame . . . or perhaps fear. It was my sister's theory that certain people couldn't *afford* to go digging up their yard on the basis of a mere rumor.

But then, Libby always made a point of agreeing with Dad, even though she sometimes missed the mark as to why.

She was alone in her support. A few times I caught even Mom giving him dark looks. Though she never said anything, those silent bursts of accusation were like the coffee spurting up in the see-through bubble on our percolator. There had been "talk" among the neighborhood wives who gathered in each other's kitchens mornings after their husbands left for work. Fortunately, the gossip didn't revolve solely around us. Near the end of August, when construction on the Cruikshanks' shelter came to a dead halt, it was whispered that Bobbie and Phil were getting divorced. No one really believed it. The D-word, as my mother called it, simply didn't apply to those of us in Hacienda Acres. Nonetheless I was sent to check it out—a mission I viewed as an act of supreme patriotism. For nothing short of the threat of being blown sky-high could have forced me next door to invite Herbie to go swimming in our Doughboy.

I wasn't the only one spying. Unlike the brand-new cars people stopped to admire—whistling in admiration as they stroked a chrome-tipped fin, and asking questions about horsepower and fuel injection that showed off their knowledge—bomb shelters were guarded with all the secrecy of wartime bunkers. No one was rushing to show off how much space they had, or the number of cans of Spam and fruit cocktail they had stockpiled. It was generally feared that when Judgment Day arrived, those who hadn't had the foresight to plan ahead would be pounding on every airtight, double-thick door to be let in. Neighbors who'd freely loaned cups of sugar and milk grew less inclined to share information that might make the difference between life or death. All of which naturally led to a certain amount of resentment.

Mr. Hardisty from up the block was caught snooping around the Millers' backyard late one night. Kids were instructed to accidentally on purpose toss their ball in so-and-so's backyard . . . and if Mrs. So-and-So wasn't home, what was the harm in retrieving it? Oh, and while you were at it, having a peek at the bomb shelter going in behind the toolshed.

My father, outspoken in his resistance to what he viewed as mob mentality, became a focus of the rumors and suspicion. Suse confided that she'd heard from a friend, who'd heard it from *her* friend, that Dad was secretly a communist. The real reason we weren't building a shelter, according to this friend of a friend, was because we were in cahoots with the Russians, and would be long gone by the time a bomb landed anywhere near us.

Tearfully, I confronted Dad. "There's a rumor going around that you're a communist." I couldn't look him in the eye, so I just sat there, picking at a scab on my knee.

"Do you believe everything you hear?" he asked.

"Not unless it's the truth." I dragged my gaze up to meet his.

"The truth?" My father paused in the midst of tamping his pipe to cast a thoughtful eye on me. Flecks of tobacco were sprinkled over the front of his cardigan and the tooled leather desk blotter that Libby and I had chipped in for last Christmas. "Well, now," he said after a moment or two, "I guess that's something we all have to find out for ourselves."

What I discovered instead was that every fad, like most rumors, passes in time. The fad that had started out as patriotism, then ballooned into paranoia, dwindled quickly into apathy. Contractors who'd been eager at first suddenly had more than they could handle. Those who stayed to finish the job demanded more money, and were fired as a result. By the time school started in the fall, there wasn't a bomb shelter on Cardinal

Place that would hold up to a stick of dynamite, much less an atomic blast.

It was during this time—with the air winey with the scent of fallen apples, and the lengthening shadows giving the ruined landscape spread out below my window the look of a lost civilization—that Mrs. Cruikshank showed up at our door late one evening. She and my mother hadn't spoken in months, not since the day Mr. Cruikshank (who'd been a little tipsy at the time) had confronted my father in the driveway and openly accused him of being a commie sympathizer. Since then Herbie's mother had made a point, if she and Mom happened to bump into each other in the supermarket, of wheeling her cart around smartly and heading in the opposite direction. The only good thing to come out of it was that Herbie had stopped pestering me. I'd see him outside, slumped dejectedly on the concrete steps that led down into the dank hole that was their unfinished shelter, and feel sorry for him almost . . . as sorry as I could for a snot-faced know-it-all who probably hadn't brushed his teeth since last Halloween.

But on that particular night Mrs. Cruikshank seemed to have forgotten that we were the enemy. Wild-eyed, she begged my parents to please, for God's sake, *do* something. It took a minute or so for the story to come out. Mr. Cruik-shank, it seemed, had had too much to drink, and they'd gotten into an argument. At the moment he was down in their bomb shelter with a shaker of martinis and a loaded gun.

I remember being terrified. I'd never seen a gun, except on TV. I tried to picture Herbie's father, overweight and losing his hair, as Hoss Cartwright . . . but from the looks on my parents' faces this was clearly no time for make-believe. I was on the verge of dashing upstairs to call Suse when the subversive thought sneaked in: *it wouldn't be fair to Herbie.*

Luckily, I was saved from having to do anything at all. Setting aside the book he'd been read-ing—*Hiroshima*, by someone named John Hersey—Dad rose from his chair. Without a word, or even so much as a hard glance, he took hold of Mrs. Cruikshank's elbow as she stood there sobbing and kneading the collar of her quilted bathrobe, and, as courteously as if asking her to dance, escorted her out the back door.

An eternity seemed to pass between the screen door slapping shut and the creak of it reopening. An eon in which my mother gave new meaning to the old expression "on the edge of her seat." It seemed the only thing keeping her from pitching face forward onto the carpet was the crochet hook clutched like a staff in one fist. My sister, as pale as the stationery on which she'd been writing to her pen pal in Australia, drifted into the kitchen to make popcorn. It was something to do, and her hands were shaking too hard to finish her letter.

We didn't know what we were waiting for. A shot maybe. Or the police sirens we were certain any minute would come screaming up our quiet street. I held my sister's buttery hand, and we prayed aloud for the first time since we were little kids, kneeling side by side at the foot of the bed in our pajamas.

But in real life, I discovered, the most dramatic events don't always end with a bang. About an hour later, Dad returned home—a bit paler than usual, maybe, but none the worse for wear. Everything was okay now, he said. He'd talked Mr. Cruikshank into giving up the gun and coming back indoors, where he and Mrs. Cruikshank had managed to get him into bed. The only indication of how tense it had been was Dad, who never swore, muttering, "One thing's for sure, he'll have a helluva hangover in the morning." He paused, as if giving himself a little mental shake, then advised calmly, "I suggest we all just sit back and take a deep breath."

Years later, I would remember that advice. When I'm tense or upset—usually over something

I can't quite put my finger on—I picture my father settling back in his La-Z-Boy with a sigh, and patting the pocket in which he kept his pipe. I would recall, too, the madness that for a brief time gripped our neighborhood—and the nation at large, I was later to learn. I'm not sure if any of us knew what a communist was . . . or if the Russians really had a bomb powerful enough to wipe every living thing off the face of the earth. I know only that one man took a deep breath and sat back.

A month after our big scare, the Cruikshanks sold their house. It was mouthed over children's heads that they'd gotten a D-I-V-O-R-C-E, and that Mrs. Cruikshank and Herbie had moved back to Ohio to be with her family. No one knew what became of Mr. Cruikshank. The new owners dug out the weed-grown ruin in back and put in a swimming pool. Summer nights, I would look out my window and see the fractured moon rippling over its dark surface . . . and from my new perspective—that of someone grown up enough to know the things that seem most real to us are often merely reflections of a much larger picture—think of poor fat Herbie.

Eileen Goudge

AFTERWORD

While my story is, for the most part, fiction, it was inspired by true-life events. Call it an homage, if you will, to a particular time and place that, for me, is the perfect metaphor of postwar American zeitgeist. I came of age in a small town on the West Coast, but in the early sixties, what was happening in our little cul-de-sac in Woodside, California, was going on in towns and suburbs across the country—a kind of mob mentality otherwise known as Cold War hysteria. We schoolchildren had been thoroughly drilled in how to save ourselves in the event of an atomic blast. It boiled down to the simplest of concepts: duck and cover. But our parents were less confident in the sturdiness of a school desk in shielding us from radioactive fallout, among other things. Thus paving the way for a curious fad (lasting roughly the average life span of a vole): the backyard bomb shelter. At one point several of our neighbors on Roan Place all had shelters under construction . . . though to my knowledge, none were ever completed. In my mind's eye, I can still peer over the fence into the Jordans' backyard and see the unfinished concrete bunker with its jutting pylons, surrounded by mounds of dirt . . . eerily like the site of an actual bomb blast. For me it symbolizes the end of an era. Good-bye hula hoops, *Leave It to Beaver,* and Campfire marshmallows in a box. Hello to the Peppermint Twist, and paranoia.

My father was among the few levelheaded holdouts to make the salient point: "What sort of life would we have in a post-apocalyptic world, anyway?" He found our neighbors' frenzy amusing for the most part. While others were ripping out patios and digging up zinnia beds to make way for bomb shelters, Daddy put in a swimming pool. In the summer kids from all over our cul-de-sac joined us in splashing our way through the last golden hours of an era, before the end of the world as we knew it.

The bomb shelters weren't a total loss, as it turned out. We found them useful for such things as slide shows, hide-and-seek, and later, spin-the-bottle. My friend Cathy claimed to have gotten her first hickey down in the dark of the Jordans' shelter. But she survived. We all did, for the most part.

Safe at Home

Eileen Dreyer

*Eileen Dreyer and Larry Helm at a
recent family get-together.*

The most amazing thing to me about my childhood was that I traversed it without having the least notion of how special my father was. In fact, I spent a lot of time being vaguely ashamed of him. After all, my father wasn't unique. He wasn't dashing or dangerous. He didn't wear jeans or cut the lawn without a shirt on. He didn't even own a gun that a kid could find tucked into a nightstand like a dirty magazine. My father was, I was afraid to admit to my friends, an accountant.

Not just an accountant, he was quick to tell us all. A CPA. A man with a degree in a neighborhood of blue collars. A solid, unpretentious calling that put enough food on the table and afforded the extras that would enable a houseful of children to attend good schools and participate in the sports they so loved.

But to a six-year-old girl whose best friend's father drove the Clydesdales and whose Uncle Bob was an undercover narcotics officer, it was tough to cloak a CPA in romance or mystery.

He used adding machines, for heaven's sake. He drove a station wagon.

I was in agony. Every parents' day. Every time I found myself on the playground engaging in another round of one-upmanship. Maggie Stevens's father had ridden the rodeo circuit for years. She had a huge silver belt buckle she kept in her crayon box to prove it. Tammie Koch's dad drove a train. And not a zoo train, either. One of the big trains, the kind we used to walk right up to, just to feel the wind of it blow our clothes against us as it went wailing past on its way somewhere we'd never been.

My father had been to Missouri and Michigan, and once he'd gone to war. In the Pacific, he said. All I knew from the blurry black-and-white pictures that curled up from Mom's black-backed scrapbook was that they must have fought that war in their underwear, which wasn't like any war I saw on television. I'm not sure that for years I even believed he hadn't made the whole thing up.

It didn't occur to me then to cherish the warm roughness of his cheek as he tucked me into bed every night, the slightly smoky scent of his shirts, or the rich bellow of his unrestrained laughter. I didn't understand how rare a thing it was to have a father who held my hand all the way into church and watched my posture there even more sharply than my mother. I didn't know that my most pristine memories would involve afternoons playing catch on the lawn or the fact that spring would always be to me the sound of Harry Carey announcing spring training games on the radio as my father bent over our old yellow Formica kitchen table teaching me to keep score.

Baseball. Oddly enough for a daughter, it was the language by which my father taught me. The language I still respond to. *Field of Dreams* and *Pride of the Yankees.* Old-fashioned heroism, team loyalty, and simple communion between a man and his child on a dirt lot as the sky turned a peacock blue at the end of a summer day.

My mother was the person who used words well. She would have been a writer in a different age, maybe a different place. She was the storyteller, the family historian, who imbued old ghosts with humor and mystery and magic. She praised with effusion and pilloried with deadly accuracy. She knew, with that terrible understanding mothers have for their children's fears and insecurities, that the most fearsome threat she could deliver for bad behavior was: "Wait till your father gets home."

And my poor father, after a day spent unraveling other people's problems, would step in the door to unravel ours. Without my mother's quicksilver epistles and trenchant parables.

My father couched his lessons in coaching lingo. And he delivered them to us all, sons and daughters alike, as if we were not simply his dependents but his team. His responsibility and his friends and his future, crouched before him with Neats' foot–oiled gloves and bright, anxious faces. He ruffled hair and smacked butts and stole noses while we weren't looking. And always he preached the tenets of the team. He taught us, his seven players, that it wasn't one of us that mattered, but all of us. That more than him, we needed each other.

He taught us the lessons that had filled his youth with magic, and filled ours with order.

And, as these things happen, it was at a baseball game I finally realized how vital this all was.

Not a real one, of course. At those I just realized that more than two hot dogs made me sick and that real baseball players cursed a lot more than my dad.

This was at a block party for our neighborhood.

We held block parties once a year in August, closing off our street and stringing Christmas lights through the trees. The local church lent tables and chairs, and one of the fathers who worked in a radio station managed to get a sound system. The mothers cooked and the children gathered games and decorations and looked forward to the night, when they could stay up under the stars that hung in their trees.

And the fathers, beer in one hand, spatula in the other, barbecued. Half-barrel, beer-marinated meat, pungent charcoal smoke that would have to be washed out of white shirts and khaki shorts. Laughing, gossiping, arguing over everything and nothing.

And in the afternoon, while the babies napped in playpens on front lawns and flies buzzed in the lazy heat, everybody would gather at the field at the end of the block for the annual baseball game.

I'm not sure why the game that particular year was different. Maybe it was because I was different, hovering uncomfortably between childhood and adolescence. Torn between the sweaty, dusty fun of shagging balls and the isolated, slightly petulant cool of standing in a group off to the side with the teenage girls.

The boys played ball until the day they died. The girls began rolling their hair and shaving their legs, and suddenly willed their ball gloves to a younger sibling. I was rolling my hair. I'd been casting covetous glances at my mother's razor. But I wanted to give myself up to the rough and tumble of a kid's game, a kid's game the fathers still played, especially on the afternoons when they barbecued in the middle of the street.

As it sometimes still does, the game won out. I untucked my new white blouse and exchanged sandals for tennis shoes and trotted over to the field that Mr. Stewart the old rodeo star was marking with base paths.

"Aw, does she have to play?" my brother Tommy asked.

My father looked up from where he was pounding home plate into the scorched grass of late summer. "And why shouldn't she?"

Tommy scowled. "Because she's a girl."

My father grinned. "Not because she's a switch hitter and bats three-fifty?"

"Three-fifty?" Mr. Stewart asked, his voice a little slurred as he stepped closer to me. "Really? You must have some arms, little girl."

For the first time I could remember, I stepped back from one of my friends' fathers. "My dad taught me," was all I said.

Mr. Stewart was really handsome. Everybody

said so. He looked like the Marlboro man, with a strong chin and light blue eyes and a swagger when he walked. We all saw him on a horse like Little Joe Cartwright or somebody, even though he just drove a truck now. But for the first time that afternoon, I noticed that his nose was red all the time. He smelled like stale beer, and his eyes, those light blue eyes that had seemed so romantic, tended to focus on places that made me nervous.

It could have been worse, I guess. I could have been on his team. But I was on Mr. Koch's team. Mr. Koch the train engineer and Mr. Stewart the ex-rodeo champ were the two managers for the day. I thought my father should have been, because, after all, he'd coached all our little league teams. He'd played baseball in high school and college, and for a while pitched for the Pat's Bar and Grill adult league team until, he said, there were too many kids for him to take the time out for weekly games.

But Mr. Koch insisted, and my dad smiled and offered to help coach. That frustrated me. After all, what good was it to have a father with one really good talent, and him not use it? Especially since Mr. Koch was such a yeller.

It might have been because he was used to needing to be heard over a train whistle. But, boy, did he yell. At everybody. He yelled at kids in the street when he was trying to get into his driveway at the end of the day. He yelled at Mrs. Koch when his dinner wasn't ready. He yelled at everybody on the grass ballfield, whether they were on his team or not. But he especially yelled at his son Timmy, who Mr. Koch decided should be pitcher.

Timmy was my friend. He was funny, and he was a great drawer and could burp the national anthem on command. But Timmy was not a pitcher. The kids on the other team cheered when they heard the news. We groaned. My dad ruffled my hair and said that wasn't the way to help a team member.

"Timmy can only pitch better if you guys all help him out," he said quietly so Mr. Koch, who was yelling at Timmy to try harder, wouldn't hear him. "Timmy needs all the encouragement he can get. So let's hear it."

Mr. Koch started assigning other positions. My brother Eddie to first base, my cousin Joey to third. Ellen Peters to right field, Mary Casey to left. Mr. Koch turned to me and began to point.

"I play shortstop," I told him, pounding my hand into my glove just like I'd seen Julian Javier on the Cardinals do it.

"Uh-huh, I'm sure," he said, already looking toward the weedy patch of field that made up center field.

Oh, no, I thought, the pleasure of playing the game dying like frogs on a driveway. I'd be sitting out in the middle of nowhere making daisy chains while the rest of them played ball, just because I was a girl.

No, I thought, catching Mr. Stewart's eye sliding my way at a moment when my dad wasn't looking. Because I was a girl who was getting breasts. It was just like school, where they seemed to think that breasts sucked out any ability to learn science or math. Well, I could understand math and science just fine. And I wanted to play shortstop.

No, what I really wanted to do was make a play at shortstop that would so surprise Mr. Koch he couldn't yell for a straight five minutes, just so he and Mr. Stewart forgot that breasts set me apart from the rest of the players.

"You'd be wasting her out in center field," my dad said to Mr. Koch as he took a sip of beer. "She's the best shortstop I've ever coached."

"That's softball," Mr. Koch said.

My dad smiled again, in that quiet way he had that made him look almost invisible, so people didn't even realize sometimes why they were doing what he wanted them to. "Try her out. It's only a game."

That was when Mr. Koch got red. Everywhere. But Mr. Koch was a redhead, and my mom said that redheads blushed faster than anybody in the world. Well, he did then. But I ended up trotting out to shortstop, right between my cousin Joey and Freddie Marston, who wore braces and carried an old Roy Rogers lunch box to school.

Mr. Koch yelled at me, of course. I was too far left, or too far right, or I wasn't crouched down low enough and might let the grounders sneak through my feet. I probably would have let it bother me if I hadn't looked over to where my father stood on the sidelines with his arm around my mom's shoulders. Because when I looked over, my dad winked. And when he winked, I remembered his biggest coaching lesson: "It's only a game." Mr. Koch, he was telling me, would never get that rule. Mr. Koch didn't like to lose. He would do anything to pull that game out. Well, anything but take out his son Timmy from pitching. But with that one wink my dad was letting me in on the joke. Mr. Koch was wasting all that energy on the perfect team for the perfect game when we were just a bunch of kids wasting time till the babies woke up and dinner was served.

"Who's gonna umpire?" my Uncle Bob asked

from where he was lying in the grass, watching the sky.

"What about you, Dad?" my cousin Joey asked.

Uncle Bob waved a hand and stayed where he was. "A man with a gun should never umpire."

We all thought that was terribly cool. I saw my mom frown and walk over to her older brother. There was some short, quiet, intense discussion that ended with Uncle Joe sitting up and my mom walking over toward the field.

"I'll umpire," she said.

All the kids cheered. My mom was a great umpire. She was always more than willing to arbitrate on the street games we'd pick up after school. And she usually never made anybody mad.

Mr. Koch looked like he was going to have a stroke, but he didn't say anything. Mrs. Marson said that Mr. Koch was afraid of my mom. After surviving my mom mad at close range more than once, I couldn't say I blamed him. But you'd think a train engineer wouldn't have much to be afraid of from a five-foot-tall housewife with seven kids. On the other hand, my dad said he was afraid of her, too. But my dad never acted like it.

"Play ball!" she yelled.

I pounded my glove a couple of times and rested my hands on my knees. Timmy reared back in the most bizarre windup anybody had ever seen and wafted a pitch a foot above Max Camper's head.

"Ball one!" Mom yelled.

The other team hooted from the old log that served as the bench. Mr. Koch started screaming. Our team, even seeing disaster loom, started chanting.

"Weenie batter, weenie batter, come on, Tim. Get this guy outa there!"

My dad, sipping his beer, smiled at my mom. My mom, who had a baby of her own on the lawn next door, smiled back. They were forever touching, my mom and dad. Hands, butts, lips. Nothing big or fancy, no sweeping anybody into a passionate embrace. Not in front of us, for sure. But they couldn't seem to walk by each other without making contact. I noticed as I watched Timmy walk the first two batters that when my Aunt Jackie brought out Uncle Bob's baseball cap, she tossed it to him from about ten feet away and then turned on her heel.

I liked Aunt Jackie. I liked Uncle Bob. But I'm not sure they liked each other. Joey was forever at our house, showing up a lot right before meals so that he'd sit down with us to eat. "There's always room for one more," my mom would say.

"Joey's on the team," my dad would answer.

"And a teammate is always welcome. Right, Joe?"

And Joey, who always looked a little nervous, like he was waiting for somebody to catch him without his homework, would take off his ball cap and sit down.

"Weenie batter . . ."

"Strike one!"

We all yelled really loudly, my dad loudest of all. Timmy had that kind of grin on his face that said he was more surprised than anyone.

"Strike two!"

Mr. Stewart was yelling now, and Uncle Bob, back to lying on the grass with a Cardinals cap over his face. And Max, finally getting the idea that Tim wasn't going to just walk him, too, swung at the ball. And hit it. Right back to Timmy, who threw it to me. Which would have been great if there'd been a runner on first.

Maybe I was the only one who noticed, but it was my dad who kept Mr. Koch from storming the field. At his own kid.

And this was just the first inning.

I didn't get my big play. Mostly what happened was that kids walked, or balls slithered by unprepared gloves into the outfield, and kids ran bases around their moms, who trotted over for congratulatory kisses. Timmy pitched, and then Eddie and then my best friend Katie, which made Mr. Koch nuts all over again. Until Katie started striking people out.

But then Katie had spent almost as many nights in my backyard as I had. Her dad was the one who drove the Clydesdales, which was really cool, because every Thanksgiving we'd all gather around the TV to watch the Macy's Thanksgiving Day parade and wave and yell to Mr. Brady, like he could hear us. He'd even invited us all down to the stables once, where they kept the horses in St. Louis, and let us sit up on top of one of the Clydesdales as if we were riding them. From that moment on, I would have been the wagon dog just to ride with them in a parade, even though that was just something else a girl couldn't do. But Mr. Brady was gone almost every day, at some parade around the country for Corn Festival or Rodeo Days or Veterans Day or something where they'd need the horses to make an appearance. Mr. Brady loved his horses. I know he loved his Katie, too, but it was my dad who taught Katie to pitch.

So I didn't get my big play. I did, however, get a big home run. It wasn't one of those mythical moments, when we were tied in the bottom of the ninth. That would have been too perfect for words. It was just in the bottom of the seventh, and we were behind three runs. Paul Bigelow was pitching for the other team, and he hated me. Which was okay, because I cheerfully hated him back. He was the neighborhood bully, and more than once he'd tried to hurt my little brothers. I'd had to knock him down. Then he'd knocked me down, of course, but the next time he tried to pull me off my bike, I ran him over. He still has a scar over his lip from where the pedal hit him.

Which meant that when I got up to bat, he tried to bean me. It didn't bother me, really, because I knew it was coming and ducked. My dad, on the other hand, wasn't amused. It wasn't just that Mr. Stewart thought it was funny. It was that it was one of Dad's kids. Heck, he got madder than my mom, and she was umping. She was also the one who'd cleaned out Paul's lip after he'd tried to run me down.

But Dad settled down when I laughed, too, because he knew that if I was okay, I'd get my evens by simply ignoring Paul's dumb move. It was sure better than clearing a bench. At least, that's what my dad thought. I just knew that laughing hurt a heck of a lot less than one of Paul's rabbit punches.

I really got my revenge on the next pitch, though. There was one man on, and Paul pitched me a perfect strike. I wound up like Stan the Man himself and corked it out into the street. I'd really like to say that nobody had ever hit a ball farther. That would be silly, since I was playing with my brother Eddie, who would go on to play for the Cincinnati Reds. But, as my dad was heard to say as he smacked me on the butt when I rounded first, "not bad for a girl." I laughed. My mom smacked my butt again when I came home. Then everybody smacked my butt. Everybody was laughing and yelling, even Mr. Koch, who for once seemed happy.

It probably would have been my best memory ever, especially since Paul looked like he'd swallowed a bug, standing out there on the pitcher's mound. But then, as I went past home, I ran into Mr. Stewart.

He'd had a beer in his hand all through the game. He had one now, and his nose was redder. His whole face was redder, and he wasn't running back and forth anymore. He seemed to move pretty fast when I jumped on home, though, because, just after my mom congratulated me, he was right in front of me, and I smacked face first into his chest.

His beer slipped and sloshed all down the front of my white shirt. His hand came out to steady me, but he seemed to need to steady me right on my left breast. And his breath was in my face, all fast and fuggy.

I bounced right back, suddenly breathing way too fast myself, but he seemed to be there, too. My stomach was upset, and I wanted to cry, even though I wasn't sure why. He was smiling. He was smiling, and his eyes had that look in them again, and suddenly everything was wrong. The day and the homer and all the people crowding around. There in the sun with my friends and my neighbors and my mom and dad, I felt crawly and afraid.

And I didn't know what to do.

So I looked over to my dad.

He must have seen something, because he was there even before I got away from Mr. Stewart's reach. His face was red, too, all of a sudden, his happy smile as gone as dinosaurs. Mr. Stewart never saw him coming, because he was looking down at me, at my shirt where the beer had splashed so you could almost see my very first bra beneath.

He didn't get the chance. Suddenly he was spun around and shuffled away, and nobody but me knew why. Nobody but me knew why he never came back out to dinner, or why he had that big bruise on his face at mass the next morning.

But I did know. I knew for sure when my dad came back ten minutes later to find me still standing there at the edge of the field, wondering what I'd done wrong. My dad walked over to me and just put his arms around me and said that Mr. Stewart had been kicked out of the game. That Mr. Stewart was no longer welcome at our home. That Mr. Stewart would never bother me again if Mr. Stewart knew what was good for him.

"I'm sorry," I whispered, reassuring myself with the slightly smoky scent of his shirt.

My dad made a funny sound in his throat, and seemed to wrap his arms around me more tightly. "No, honey. Mr. Stewart is sorry. It's his fault and his fault alone. He forgot for a minute that you aren't an adult. He won't forget again. And if anybody . . . *anybody* . . . ever makes you feel the way you felt today, you just let me know. That's what I'm there for."

I pulled away a little, so I could look up at him. Just to make sure. To see that my mom was waiting for her turn just past him.

"You mean it?" I asked, all over shaking again because, for the first time in my life, I saw tears in my father's eyes, and that scared me almost more than Mr. Stewart's hand on my breast.

"Oh, yeah, honey," my dad said, and kissed the

top of my head. "After all, I'm the coach. I watch out for my team, don't I?"

And in that moment I realized that CPAs were cooler than cowboys, than train engineers. Even than the guys who drove the Clydesdales. Because standing there at the edge of my childhood, with summer behind me and my dad's arms around me, I felt safe. I felt secure and warm and cherished. And I knew that no matter what else my dad did or didn't do, what clothes he wore or people he knew, he knew how to raise a team. And that his kind of coaching was all I needed to take me on, and take me through.

And it has. Especially now that I have a team of my own.

AFTERWORD

The story is fiction. I had no Uncle Bobby, none of my friends' fathers drove a train (although I did, in fact, once, get to sit on a Clydesdale). We did have block parties and ballgames when I grew up, but none ended like this one. But the character of my father does indeed infuse the story. He is a CPA (and proud of it), he and my mom did raise a big family with love and respect, and he was one of the greatest Khoury League coaches in town. To that, my story is true. And to the base-ball. As a matter of fact, it was at the game in which Mark McGwire broke the home run record that I taught my own daughter to keep score.

Raised as His Own

Billie Sue Mosiman

*Billie Sue Mosiman at Carlsbad Caverns
with her daddy and mama on
the day of their marriage.*

I didn't choose my father, he chose me. My biological father and mother divorced when I was a baby. I never met the man. I was told after I was grown that my biological father kept a baby picture of me in his wallet and he grieved that my mother wouldn't allow contact between us. Indeed, the baby photo was on him the day he had a head-on collision while driving to work. We might have loved one another if we'd been together, but we weren't, not even for a day, and that wasn't as sad as it might seem.

My stepfather, my real father, came along when I was two. He fell in love, so absolutely and completely in love. The moment he discovered she had a child, he said to her, without hesitation, "If you'll marry me, your little girl will be raised as my own."

Raised as my own. That means nothing to anyone but the child it refers to and the father who promises to do it.

How many people say such a thing and really mean it? Mean it for a lifetime, mean it forever? I don't think too many. And even if they mean it at the time, how many follow through on a lifelong promise? Even fewer.

But my father meant it, and he has followed through all the way. He never made me feel I was unloved, unwanted, or not his own. I was his, all right.

My first memories of him are of a tall, lean man with wavy brown hair and blue eyes. A handsome fellow with a slow smile, an even slower temper, and a sly wit. In his late twenties he began to lose his hair, began to go bald, but what remained was still silky and wavy and quite beautiful. I looked up to him, so tall above me, and wondered if he would be mine and I would be his. If the arrangement would last. If this was the daddy I needed so much.

He had been in the Navy, at Pearl Harbor, but he never talked about what happened there during the bombing. The past was a thing best left behind. He moved steadily into the future, taking on a family right away, settling down to make a life for them. He knew Morse code, so his first job was with the telegraph company on the railroad. In a few years, and after going to night school for accounting, he got on with the Gulf Oil Company, where he stayed even when it was bought by Texas Eastern.

He delighted in my childhood and made it fun. I remember drive-in movies, picnics, milkshakes at the Dairy Queen, family barbeques, and baseball games. I remember him taking me onto his shoulders into deep Gulf waters off the Galveston, Texas, beach, and I was secure that he would not let me go; he wouldn't let me drown. The sun sparkled off the water, the waves came in smooth and slow. Daddy went in over his head, paddling along, and there I sat queenly on his shoulders, unafraid.

One summer when at the beach and I was wading in knee-high water, jellyfish surrounded me, wrapping around my legs and ankles. It was instant agony. I was screaming when Daddy came running to scoop me into his arms and shake off the monsters. He was the one who doctored the fiery red marks and the one who talked to me softly to still my fear, my panic, my pain. I learned that he would be there to keep me afloat and be there when I was in trouble.

One day when I made a bow and arrows out of tree branches and shot down a wasps' nest hanging from the eave of the house, and the wasps outran me to sting my flesh silly through my socks and sandals, it was Daddy who applied the damp baking soda, and Daddy who warned me that messing around with Mother Nature nearly always results in dire reprisal.

If I had a toothache, Daddy put something on it. If I had a splinter, Daddy took it out. And if I did something wrong, though that was seldom, Mama always let Daddy handle it when he came home from work.

Fathers come in so many shades and permutations. There is the Too-Strict Father and the Easygoing Dad. The Demanding Father, the Pushy Dad, the Dad-with-No-Time-for-You. There are Cold Fathers and Smothering Fathers, fathers who are barely there in spirit, fathers who wish you had never been born or at least never had any connection to them whatsoever.

My father is one of those rare species—a guy who knows exactly what his job is: His role as my father was to be there, and he never shucked that responsibility. He is, for want of a better description, an Old-Fashioned Dad.

During the early years when he and my mother had their disagreements, even separations, Daddy didn't give up me or my brother. He never stopped being our father. It would have been an easy thing to do, convenient. The woman kept leaving him. Maybe he should let the kids go too, if it was going to be that way. Yet I doubt the idea ever once occurred to him. He didn't file for a divorce, never even threatened to. He'd see this thing through. He had married my mother, and although they might be having their problems, that had nothing to do with his role and responsibility as my father. I might spend the summer, or even a year or more, with my grandparents. Or my mother might take me with her to another city, move out of his house, wouldn't be in touch with him for months on end. But he was still my father.

I used to think, well, he and Mama are arguing and separated, I guess I don't have a dad anymore. But after the very first time that happened, I learned differently—much to my relief. I'd already lost one father. How many would I have to lose anyway? Daddy wasn't going to let me find out. He was *it*. He was my father, no matter what happened, no matter where I lived or with whom. Whenever I spoke the word "Daddy," it meant him and never would mean anyone else.

In Helena, Arkansas, there were quite a few lessons to be learned from my father. And it was there when it was strongly pointed out to me that I had a different name from my parents. The first day of school the principal took me into my homeroom and introduced me. Then she handed over my school transcript and papers to the teacher and left the room. I stood there beside the desk, scared and unhappy. I'd been in so many schools in so many states. It was always frightening.

The teacher looked up from my papers and said, "Your name is Billie Sue Stahl?" I nodded yes, that was my name. (In earlier grades children called me "billy goat" and "cow stall." Charming how children know how to muck up your name, isn't it?) She said, "Then why are your parents' last name Smith?"

My face reddened. It was 1959 and, as odd as it sounds today, when half of all marriages end in divorce, not many children had divorced parents. I said, "Their name is Smith because my dad is my stepdad."

The other kids in the class might have winced or looked away or looked upon me with pity, but I wouldn't know because I couldn't look at them to see. I felt ashamed, as if I had done something wrong. I was an outcast, without my own real father at home. I had a name that belonged to no one else in my family. Why did this teacher have to bring it up now, on my first day, and make me a pariah in the school?

Then I hated her. I knew with certainty that my family was just as normal as any other family and that my name was fine and it was okay that I had a stepfather.

What they didn't know is they didn't have to pity me. I had a daddy, a good one, one I loved and who loved me. It didn't matter about the name. He'd even discussed with my mother adopting me and giving me his name, but they decided it wasn't necessary. What's a name got to do with being a father?

So in Helena for the first time I discovered that having a divorced and remarried mother was not the usual family circumstance. But I also knew there was nothing wrong with it, and people who thought there was were merely narrow-minded and ignorant.

My birthday came along not long after school let out. If I could wheedle Daddy into it, I could get something to make up for the rough times during the school term. I wanted a transistor radio. I wanted it more than anything ever, ever, ever. Transistors had just come out, and they were costly. They were small enough to fit into the palm of the hand, made of cheap plastic, ate up battery power like crazy, and brought in only a couple of AM stations. But they were portable! I could listen to it at night in my bed. What an incredible luxury that would be. I begged Daddy for months before my birthday. "I really want it,

Daddy. I have to have it." I'd never really asked for something before. Not anything I really wanted that much. He had to understand.

On my birthday I thought my heart would leap out of my chest as I opened my present. It was the radio! A little turquoise blue plastic box. And it worked, oh, how it worked. I listened to it every night, thrilling to the music of Elvis Presley and Otis Redding and Johnny Cash. I loved it more than anything. Music to put me to sleep. Music to listen to while the family watched television. Music when I was riding my bike!

Then the little radio broke. Probably from having been mashed against my ear on some night filled with nightmares that caused me to toss and turn. I was sick at heart. "Daddy, can we fix it?" I asked.

He said he'd take it to the radio shop and see what they could do.

That's what you did back in the fifties. You took things to a fix-it shop and had them repaired. The radio probably cost close to sixty dollars, and you didn't just run out and replace it.

Two weeks went by, and then one day Daddy came home and said, "There's bad news about your radio."

"What?"

"The shop that was repairing it burned to the ground yesterday."

"Oh, no, my radio, Daddy, what about my radio?"

"Everything was lost. But the shop owner's going to pay me some money for the loss of the radio from his insurance."

I naturally thought Daddy would buy me another one. Of course he would. He had to know how much I loved it, right?

I'm afraid not. I waited and waited and finally, a couple months later, Daddy came home with a box for me. But it was too small. Could he have found an even smaller transistor radio? I ripped open the package, excitement and happy anticipation causing me to tingle all over. Inside the box was . . . a wristwatch. I had never been so disappointed. It was a great watch. It had little diamond chips and twenty-one jewels. An Elgin. Any young girl would have been proud to own it and to show it off. But I didn't care a fig for watches. I loved radios, didn't Daddy know that?

I looked at his face and realized he hadn't a clue. He thought I'd like the watch more. A watch meant that I was grown-up enough to take care of it. It meant I would be on time and I would always know when I was to be home for dinner. I hadn't the heart to tell him a beautiful watch could never in a million years replace a radio. Instead, I put the watch on my wrist, pretended to admire it, and told him how pretty it was.

I guess that's why today I own more portable radios than any one sane person ought to. It's overcompensation, I know, but you never get over losing a birthday present you loved so much when you were eleven. Trust me, *never.*

Despite losing the transistor radio, Daddy made sure I was supplied with a weekly allowance so that I could indulge in buying 45 rpm records and comic books. These things *almost* made up for the loss.

It was later that summer when a young male cousin came to stay with us awhile. He stole a sock filled with pennies that belonged to my brother. We all knew it. What we didn't know was what to do about it. Daddy stepped in and took the boy aside where they would be in private. I learned later that he simply had a little talk with him. Daddy was never very physical with us. (And when he was, we really deserved it. Like the time when I was sixteen and talked back to my mother, refusing to wash the dishes. I'd stepped over the line, and, boy howdy, did Daddy let me know it.)

Out of the bedroom came my cousin with his head hanging and a sad look on his face. He went to where he'd hidden the sock of money, retrieved it, and handed it over to my brother with an apology. You don't steal in our house. That was the rule, we all knew that. Lying, stealing, not going along with the program . . . absolutely out of the question.

Another time in Helena our dog, Lady, came down sick. Back then dogs weren't given vaccinations the way they routinely are today. Lady had distemper. She grew sicker and sicker, her poor brown eyes glazing over and her movements slowing. I said to Daddy, "Can you fix Lady?" He explained that he couldn't, unfortunately, and that we were most probably going to lose her. And we did. One day she was lying under the tree behind the house. Daddy picked her up so gently and carried her away to bury. I appreciated that about Daddy. How he just handled things that needed handling, and with as little fuss and bother as possible so the people involved weren't forced to deal with hysterical emotions on top of a loss.

It was in Helena, too, where Daddy let my brother and I go to the matinees in town every Saturday. Oh, we'd been given that treat every Saturday everywhere we lived, for just as long as I could remember. I think the majority of youngsters in America attended the Saturday matinees. It was a matinee in Helena, when I had just turned twelve, that I met a boy at the movie house. We saw one another there every weekend, sitting together, sharing popcorn. One Saturday he put his arm around my shoulder, and once, just once, he leaned over to plant a quick kiss on my lips. Then he gave me his sterling silver name bracelet.

My first boyfriend. And we were "going together."

Until I came home from the theater and forgot to take off the bracelet and hide it from Daddy's gaze. I was down on the floor, reading a book, when he pointed at my wrist and asked, "What's that?"

Oh, too late to hide it, too late, too late! Now he'd kill me.

"It's nothing," I lied, trying to hide my arm behind my leg.

"Let me see it," he said.

"But, Daddy, it's just a bracelet."

"Let me see it."

When you have an Old-Fashioned Dad, you don't disobey him if you know what's good for you. I slipped the clunky, too-big bracelet off my wrist and handed it over. I couldn't look at him. I felt all hot and ashamed and scared inside. Even I knew I was too young to have a boyfriend. And now I'd been caught. I'd been secretive. I'd broken an unspoken family rule of honesty and forthrightness.

Daddy scrutinized the bracelet and read the name aloud. I think it said DONNY. It was a long time ago. "Who's Donny?" he asked.

So I had to explain that I'd met this boy at the movies and he gave it to me. My brother, sneaking into the living room and noting my terror, chimed in, "He was kissing her!"

"Did not!" I screamed. Oh, it was very hard to have a younger brother some days, very hard.

"Did, too! Daddy, he puts his arm around her shoulders, and I saw him kiss her, I *saw* him."

Daddy said nothing, no lecture. He quietly handed the bracelet back to me, and he simply said, "Give it back. You can't have a boyfriend yet. You're too young."

That's all he had to say. That's all he had to do. His job was to tell me the right way, teach me the right things, help me grow up right. The next Saturday I gave the bracelet back, and I never sat with the boy again. I don't remember feeling too badly about it, either. Donny was awfully cute, but it was very difficult to have to sit with him all the time and be his girl and no one else's. Why, that was just stupid, and although I'd really liked kissing, I figured I could wait for all that.

You see, I think Daddy knew everything. He knew when I took Donny's bracelet that I didn't really want to have a boyfriend. He was right.

Why spank me or punish me or ground me when all he had to do was handle things and let me figure out on my own when I had done wrong? He knew I knew better. He had some faith in me. That's what good Old-Fashioned Fathers are like.

What I always loved most as a kid around Daddy was his sly sense of humor. He might say something to us in a regular tone of voice and with a straight face, but *what* he said was as funny as all get-out. It might be a play on words or a pun; it might be a joke or a twist to the logic of a situation. We might not cotton to it right away. There was always a delay (and still is) of a few seconds after Daddy was "being funny" and the moment recognition hit us and we'd laugh our heads off. When he thought we were being funny, he'd call us "goofy outfits." Or he'd say, "We don't need to hear from the peanut gallery."

And sometimes he thumped our heads if we weren't being funny but acting like outright pests. Not mean thumps. Just good solid, have-I-got-your-attention? thumps. We'd rub our scalps and say, "Aw, Daddy! Goll-ly."

Daddy was sly. Quiet, reserved, not particularly a huggy-type dad. Funny, understanding, and resolute. He knew all about being funny and being serious and when it was appropriate to choose between the two.

145

He knew his job. You had to know yours. As his child you were expected to mind your elders, don't talk back, don't give lip, be morally correct, and keep your wits about you. It wasn't all that much to ask. He was raising human beings to live in a civilized world where manners counted and honesty was rewarded.

I was back and forth to Helena. The last time I was back was when I was in the eleventh grade. Class ring time. They were expensive. Daddy always had a good job with the oil companies, but this ring—it wasn't going to be cheap. I wanted that ring. I wanted it more than anything—well, not quite as much as I'd wanted the transistor radio, but then there's nothing I ever wanted more than that. But if I didn't get the class ring and if I went back to Alabama that same year, I'd miss out on getting a ring from *any* high school. I'd be the only senior without a class ring.

I wondered, though, if we could afford it. I didn't beg for the ring or even say much about it. But one day Daddy handed over a ring box and there it was. A red stone in the center, a real gold band.

In later years I wondered what Daddy did without to get that ring for me. Did he miss some lunches, scrimp on a bill that needed paying? I never knew, but I did know it was something that he probably had to sacrifice to get for me and it meant something—more than if he'd been a rich man, giving me everything I asked for or thought I wanted.

When my parents were transferred to upstate New York, I had to go along. I'd been in my senior year in Alabama, but it was time to be with my folks again and New York was it. I loved the Catskill Mountains, Albany, trips into New York City, the gorgeous spring fields of wildflowers, the glorious array of fall leaves, but school was a real drag. Even the teachers made fun of my Southern accent, and I was not assimilating into the crowd. I went to Daddy. "Can I go back and finish school in Alabama?" I asked. "I want to go to the University of Alabama anyway, and if I stay here, I'll be an out-of-state resident. It'll cost a lot more."

Daddy let me return to my grandparents and the place I thought of as home, Alabama.

After graduation I went back to spend the summer in New York and worked to save money for college back in Alabama. Although I was taking out a government student loan and meant to work my way through college, Daddy supplied ten dollars a week, every single week, for extra spending money. One of my first summer jobs was at a root beer stand in Albany. Daddy faithfully drove me to work and picked me up afterward. I hadn't been there a week when the manager told me I had to sew up the hem of my skirt—shorten it considerably. We waited on cars, taking trays to the windows, and I guess this guy thought legs sold root beer. He was right, I'm sure, but I was a demure young woman at the time and did not take kindly to the idea I should play on my feminine wiles to boost business. When Daddy came to pick me up, I told him about it on the way home. "How do you feel about that?" he asked.

"I don't like it. I don't want to make my skirt shorter. He bugs me about it all the time, Daddy, he's driving me crazy."

"Okay."

He never said anything else, and I didn't know what it all meant until he took me back to work the next day. He came in with me and asked to see the manager. I stood there, proud and a little surprised, while he said, "My daughter does not want to wear short skirts to work. If that's a prerequisite for this job, then I'll just take her home with me now. I don't really think you have a right to force anyone to shorten the uniform."

The manager backed down and never bothered me again. I guess he knew a father who meant business when he met one.

I stopped going to New York after two summers. In fact, I quit college the end of my sophomore year to go traveling. It was 1967, and it seemed everything in the world was happening in San Francisco. The hippie movement, free love, drugs and rock 'n' roll. I had to go there. I had to see for myself. Every young person in the country knew something was afoot, something was changing. If I missed out seeing it up close, being a part of it, then I'd never forgive myself. I meant to be a writer, and I knew writers had to experience the world in ways others might wish to sidestep or ignore.

Once I got to San Francisco and spent a week roaming among the disenfranchised youth there, I figured it wasn't my scene, as it were. I was no more fit for Haight-Ashbury than that New York high school. So I drifted on down to Long Beach, outside L.A. And there met my husband-to-be.

I was twenty-one and in love. My mother, sure that I should not be in wild and evil California on my own, called to say my brother had been in a car accident. "Come home," she pleaded. That same night I answered my boyfriend's proposal with a yes. The next day he gave me a wedding ring set, and we made plans to be married two weeks later in New York. It wasn't until I arrived home on a cross-continent plane trip that I discovered my mother had exaggerated my brother's injuries from the accident. Just to get me back home. I had returned, it seemed, for a broken nose.

Nevertheless, when I came off the plane, Daddy was waiting. I hadn't told my parents a thing about being in love. It had all happened so quickly, in a flash, that I hardly had time to take it all in myself. But my excitement was so high I couldn't hold it in any longer. I held out my left hand. "Look," I said, spreading my fingers, watching the little diamond sparkle.

"What's that?"

"It's an engagement ring. I'm going to get married."

Imagine the moment, July 1968. Your daughter, who did so well in school and in college decided to drop out and join the counterculture. (Or that's the way it appeared.) Then within months she's home with a ring on her finger and talking about getting married. The daughter who told you she didn't care about boys and marriage, and certainly not babies and housework! The daughter who had a dream of being a writer, who wanted to travel and experience whatever the world had to offer. The daughter Who Would Be Great. She Who Would Amount to Something.

And she wants to get married. Never go back

to college. Marry and no doubt have babies and ruin her whole life.

But Daddy was, and is yet, nonjudgmental. It's his gift. He did not say anything either in favor or disfavor of the marriage, not then in the airport. On the way home he discussed with me how Mama would react. Not well, we both agreed. It was going to be a real shock. We were going to need stamina for this.

After the shock and the acceptance that yes, indeed, I was serious and I was going to get married, Mama set about making plans. Daddy bought a dress that cost a thousand dollars. He ordered flowers for the church. He paid for a photographer for the event and reserved a room for us in Lake George for our honeymoon.

But one of the nights before my fiancé, Lyle, was to arrive from California, Daddy and I were alone at the kitchen table and I could see it was time for The Talk.

"Are you sure about this?"

"I'm sure, Daddy."

"Does he have savings?"

"Ummm, I don't know. I don't think so."

"He's been in the Navy nearly five years and he has no savings? What will you live on?"

"Oh, I'll work too."

"I thought you wanted to be a writer."

"I'll work and write at the same time. Lots of people have done it."

"Have you met his parents?"

"No. They live in Michigan, and we'll go see them after the wedding, on the way back to California."

"So you don't know what they're like?"

"No, but I'm not marrying his parents."

"That's true. What about college? I thought you were going back."

"I probably won't. We'll live in Long Beach another year until he's out of the Navy. But I won't stop learning. I won't stop writing. I'll still be a writer, Daddy."

He seemed satisfied with my answer. Or perhaps he thought all potential writers were as crazy as this. "All right, let me ask you a question."

"Sure. Anything."

"How do you know you love him? You've only known him two weeks."

"Daddy, I'm twenty-one. I've lived on my own for three years, had my own apartment, worked at jobs, saved money, and traveled alone. I've had boyfriends. I never felt about anyone the way I feel about Lyle. I can't stand to be away from him. I think I might even die without him. I know I love him. And, Daddy?"

He nodded for me to continue.

"He's a lot like you."

"Is he?" And then he smiled.

"A lot. He works hard, and I know he'll always take care of me. He's funny, he makes me laugh. I don't think he ever gives up on things. I think he's loyal. I think he's a good man."

Daddy soaked that in and was silent for a few minutes. Then he said, "All right. I guess you really love him."

I leaped up and hugged my father. He understood it. He knew it was right for me, it wasn't a mistake, and that I would be happy.

It wouldn't be truthful to say that I never have disagreed or had arguments with my father. But they were few and far between. Over the years I've always felt I could just tell him anything and it would be all right. When my first novel was about to be published, I worried that my father, a man raised by a Nazarene preacher, a man who never used profanity, would find the raw language in my book disgusting. I had to warn him before he saw it in print.

"Daddy, now when *Wireman* comes out, you have to know something before you read it."

"What's that?"

"Well, you know it's about these two guys, they're brothers, and they were in Vietnam."

"Yes?"

"And . . . well, when they talk, they say some bad words. You know. Profanity."

Daddy surprised me. "Oh, I know men in the service cuss. It wouldn't be like real people if they didn't. I don't see anything at all wrong with that."

I know I must have let out a heavy breath. Nonjudgmental. A good man. He knew I was going to have to write the world as I saw it, and if a character said something ugly or did something monstrous, well, that's how I'd write it. In fact, *Wireman* continues to be my father's favorite novel of mine. I don't think I ever had anything to worry about. Of everyone in the family, my father is the only one who has read every single book I have published. He doesn't crow or brag on me, doesn't make a big deal of it, but he reads the books. That's the most important thing of all.

Daddy spent his entire life working hard. He finally retired here to Texas, where my brother and I live, and bought a marina-campground on a lake. A few years ago he had a heart attack and was diagnosed with a damaged heart. He underwent quadruple-bypass heart surgery. No fuss, no hysterics. Yes, he was a diabetic and had to use insulin injections. Yes, he understood the diabetes had caused his heart damage and even after the surgery his arteries would probably clog up again. Yes, he knew this was serious and dangerous and all of that, but let's get on with it, gentlemen, let's get the work done.

Let's all do our jobs.

He came out of the hospital and stayed a week with me during recovery. I helped him move around, brought him food, and listened to what he said to be sure he wasn't getting depressed. My father, depressed! Not likely. He had everything to live for. His retirement years, his wife, me, my brother, his grandchildren and great-grandchildren.

It was but a year of good health before his arteries began to close down again. They couldn't operate a second time, and none of the other procedures would do any good either. He was put into an experimental drug program, where he didn't know if he was given the new drug or a placebo, but he did it anyway. His diabetes gets out of control often, so that his sugar level swings up and down. He's lost weight and can't do nearly as much around the marina as he used to. He likes to sit in his recliner and watch the Cowboys play football. He likes to see us come visit, to play dominoes with him, and card games. He is a Republican and enjoys a good argument with his less conservative children.

My brother and I have suggested that he sell the place and buy a little house closer to where we both live. The marina's a hundred miles distant. If he lived closer, we could see about him, help out more, and he'd be near his doctors. But Daddy puts it off. He sank his retirement money into the place, and it's his home. All those years of transfers with the oil companies seems to have worn him out on moving. He likes sitting still for a while now. He and Mama get along pretty well there yet. He's not ready to give anything up. I don't think he ever will.

What does a man do who has spent his life living up to all his responsibilities? He has always been steadfast. He never missed a day of work. He never got fired. He saved his money and cared for his family. He was a bookkeeper, an accountant, and a good one. He did not live a lifestyle or indulge in habits that gave him diabetes and a bad heart. These are things visited on him without his help. And because age is coming on and his illness is deepening, does he simply give up all that he has, change his life, become semi-dependent on children he raised? Not my daddy. Whether it would be better for him or not is not the question. Whether he could stand it, that is the question, and one should never ask a man to be other than the man he is.

My father is a good one. A kind, understanding, nonjudgmental, optimistic, steadfast father. He chose me. And I have chosen him. We were lucky, he and I. Fate sent him to my mother and into my life. He took me to him and has kept me fast. I never put up a photograph of my biological father. I never knew the man, or loved him. I have a photograph of my father in my house. I know this man.

And I love him.

And if I could wish anything for a young child who cannot for some reason be with a biological father, I wish that there is a real father waiting for her somewhere. Fathers are not created by the blood, as we have always presumed.

Fathers reside in the heart.

Part Two

———∞∞∞———

Coming to Terms

Semi-Precious Memories

Marilyn Reynolds

Marilyn Reynolds and her father, Lester Fay Dodson, as they began the walk down the aisle of the Temple City Baptist Church, March 25, 1956.

Unpacking books in our new house, I come across *Tuckaway House*, first published in 1926. As I open the book and flip randomly through the pages of the first chapter, my father's presence fills the room. A sudden sensation, a sensation of body rather than mind, transports me back to the age of eight, a time when I was a daddy's girl, and the apple of my father's eye. I am curled up next to him in his big, overstuffed chair, and he is reading to me as he did most evenings after dinner. He has a bottle of beer on the table next to him, and next to that is my small glass of beer, a glass that once held Kraft pimento cheese, the Brie of the forties. Now, four hundred miles and fifty-five years away from that scene, the aroma of tobacco smoke and beer, with a hint of laundry starch from his white shirt, permeates my being and I let myself sink into the past.

When reading to me, my father never stuck to the story, and as I skim the *Tuckaway House* account of Dicey, the old colored cook who had "been in the family ever since Mother was born," I can imagine him pausing and telling me about the "old mammy" who had been much loved by him and his brothers and sisters. He would have told me a funny story, laughing about how Mammy was afraid of Pal, the mule, because she was convinced it harbored evil spirits. He probably would have gone on to tell me how much better off the coloreds were in the times when they lived with white families who loved them and took care of them. I would have believed him then, because I was only eight, and he was still my hero, and he had not yet been decimated by the power of alcohol.

On impulse, I bury my face in the pages of *Tuckaway House*, attempting to increase the sense of my father's presence, but instead I am thrown into a sneezing fit that brings me back to the reality of my day.

I dust, then shelve *Tuckaway House*, and get on with the task at hand, leaving my father behind. *Word Menu*, *Writer's Digest*, *Bird by Bird*, *Warriner's English Grammar and Composition*, some of the tools of my writing trade go on the shelf over my computer; then I move on to general fiction. Box after box sits waiting to be unpacked. It is an overwhelming task, this moving from a home of twenty-five years.

Late in the day, I find several soft, leather-bound books of poetry by Edgar A. Guest, and my father shows up again. " 'When Day Is Done,' " he announces in his soft, Southern-flavored voice. I can sense his stubby fingers readying themselves to treat the thin, fluttery pages with careful respect. The poem is about a man who, at the end of the day, reaches his garden gate, where his children are waiting, and tells himself "That life is good and its tasks worth while. . . ."

Again I revisit the childhood pleasure of nestling next to my father in his big easy chair and letting his words wash over me like a warm, crooning rain.

I can't put a date on when we lost each other. By the time I was fourteen I had, predictably, begun to notice his imperfections. He was unreasonable in matters regarding race, threatening to withdraw me from the neighborhood school when he heard the new teacher there was a black woman. He was hard on Dale, my five-year-old brother—always wanting him to fight back, be a man, not cry when the bully across the street beat him up, not sleep with his teddy bear.

Probably the drink was getting to him even

then, though at the time I thought I'd never seen my father drunk. I'd seen my uncle Dave drunk, dancing around the living room with a burning log in his hand, claiming to be an Apache as sparks flew and my slightly less drunk aunt tried to stomp them out. I'd seen some of my father's friends drunk—those hardworking, poker-playing, crap-shooting, horse-betting characters who always had kind words or a story for me. I knew what drunk was, and it was nothing I'd ever seen in my steady father. Then, when I was fifteen, my father bet a large sum of money that he could quit drinking. He had a certain gambler's pride, and would never renege on a bet, so he was without alcohol for a month. That's when I realized I had probably never seen him sober. It's not that his personality changed drastically; it's just that there was more of it, more of him.

When his month-long bet was up, he savored a cold beer and said he would never go back to the "other stuff." "Never" lasted a day or two. I was mildly disappointed to see the shots of whiskey reappear, though I brought no judgment against him in my teenage heart. We laughed together. He was unfailingly pleased to see me when I dropped by his market, Dodson's Choice Meats, or when I came in late from a date to find him sitting in his chair, smoking, a drink on the table beside him. In those days he was trying to figure out what to do about his failing business—how to make things better, how to turn things around, how to compete with the big guys selling on narrow margins.

It was not until I was grown and married, and he had been diagnosed with the beginnings of cirrhosis, that I understood the seriousness of his drinking habits. That's how I thought of it. A habit. Not a disease, or an addiction, but a habit, and one he could control if he would only exert a little willpower. I knew that his own father had died in his fifties, in the midst of a periodic binge. Uncle Bill, who might have held the record for length of sequential months lived in a state of drunkenness, died at forty-one. Uncle Otis, Uncle Earl, Uncle Roy, Uncle Hugh, Uncle Goode, were all either alcoholics or reformed alcoholics. Aunt Gladys, Aunt Willie, Aunt Dot, all drank to the extent that it sometimes had serious consequences for them. The only one of my father's siblings who had not at one time or another had a big-time drinking problem was Aunt Ruth, who never once tasted alcohol. Of the eleven children in my father's family, she was the only one who had taken heed of their dissipated father's admonition to never touch the stuff.

During my growing-up years, in addition to reading together, my father and I played checkers and fake-boxed and played catch. He taught me how to play poker, how to be aware of what cards were on the table and what might be lurking in the hole, and he taught me how to read the tote board at the races. But our very favorite pastime, to my mother's everlasting consternation, was arguing. One of our typical Sunday dinner arguments when I was in my teens and working at thinking for myself was in the nurture-nature realm. *Environment* and *heredity* were the terms used in the fifties. I claimed then that environment was the most important influence on a person's life, and my father held that heredity was the major factor.

We could argue endlessly, each tossing out convincing anecdotal evidence, but neither of us ever looked at the drinking patterns of my father's family as we pursued our subject. As obvious as it seems now, in light of all of the research and insight regarding addiction and genetic coding, neither of us considered that alcoholism lurked in the family gene pool. For all of my father's belief that heredity determined a person's physical and intellectual traits, a belief that supported his racist slant on life, he had a stronger, less obvious belief in free will. Perhaps that belief was never placed on the dining room table because it was a belief we shared. If we couldn't argue about it, why discuss it? But it was the certainty of his free will, that he could stop drinking if only he would choose to, that turned me from him in disgust.

I was twenty-four, pregnant with my second daughter, the first time my father was hospitalized. A nose bleed, my mother said when she called. It was a three-day hemorrhage that required packing and suturing to stop. This time his doctor, the doctor who played poker and drank with him, told him it was time to stop drinking. Scared, he quit for a few weeks. But my mother gave her own continual medical advice, easier for him to believe than Dr. Greer's, that just one drink now and then couldn't hurt. Probably the pull of alcohol would have overcome him whatever her advice, but in my heart I held her partly responsible when he started in again.

From the time of that first hospitalization to the time of his death, my father was on a steady, obvious decline. I would watch him, muzzy and addled, reach for another drink, and I would hate him for it. Whenever I tried to talk with him about it, he would agree that it just took a little willpower, and he would cut back, or quit, or whatever words seemed right to him at the time.

But he could never make good on his stated intentions. When my brother and I urged my mother to quit drinking, quit having it in the house, she would cry and say it was all they did for entertainment and ask how we could begrudge them that one pleasure.

Dale and I watched as our father became less and less coherent, less and less steady on his feet. Even with subsequent hospitalizations, when he'd dried out for a few days, his speech was tongue-heavy and he needed to hang onto things to get from one side of the room to the other. Once home from the hospital it would all start again. He fell and broke his kneecap. He had a bleeding ulcer. His hands shook so that he could barely light a cigarette. He could no longer break down a side of beef. Old friends pitched in to help him keep his small market open—the one he'd moved to after he'd lost the battle with Alpha Beta and Safeway. Still he drank.

At times when he could not get out of bed, my mother would drive to the liquor store and bring back a pint of Early Times. When that was gone, often only a few hours later, she would go to a different store for another pint. They never bought in quantity, not seeing themselves as big drinkers.

I continued to try to talk to him, though the

Sunday dinners were over for me and my daughters. I told my mother that if they were determined to drink themselves to death I couldn't stop them, but we weren't going to watch the process Sunday after Sunday. Minus the Sundays, I continued to see my parents often, for short periods of time, and got daily reports of my father's condition.

Every time I entered my childhood home, I was overcome with a sense of loss and futility. The books of poetry still sat beside my father's chair. The contours of his once healthy body were still apparent in the worn cushions. But *he* was not there. More and more I observed the agonizing scenes of his last years as if I were in a dreamlike state, floating, ungrounded. With my children, students, friends, I was fully engaged. But I kept my father locked in a psychic compartment where he could not contaminate the rest of my life.

The father who had read to me and laughed with me was so far removed from the father of the later years that my strongest emotion at his death was not grief or loss, but relief. I'd seen him the night before, waited for each exhalation, knowing he was dying but not exactly believing it. There had been so many close calls, so many warnings. But early the next morning my mother called.

"Your daddy's gone," she said in a sort of uneven whisper.

I don't remember my outward reply. My guess is it seemed appropriate to her. But my inner voice fairly screamed, "Thank God *that's* over."

At the funeral I shook hands and shared hugs with my father's old friends. "A good man," they said, "honest as the day is long." Some told of how my father had loaned them money when they were down and out, or let them stay at our house, or put extra meat in the package for the man who couldn't afford enough to feed his whole family. I watched my father's seventy-year-old sister crumble in tears as she saw the coffin settled into the grave. "My baby brother. My baby brother," she sobbed over and over again. And I kept my relief to myself.

All through the handshakes and hugs and stories and tears, my private mantra played as if coming to me from an old, cracked 78. "Thank God it's over; thank God it's over; thank God it's over. . . ." Later, when my mother suggested that we have BELOVED HUSBAND AND FATHER engraved on his marble headstone, I agreed, though my heart was as hard as the very marble that would have the sweet words chiseled into it. For me, it would have seemed more appropriate to carve

"Thank God it's over" into the waiting stone. But it wasn't over.

Two years after his death, sometime toward the end of 1968, my father came sneaking in through the Ouija board that my brother and I were playing around with. I was then pregnant with my third child, and Dale was in graduate school. I'm sure we both had other ways to spend our time, but on that hot summer day we were dabbling in phantom realms. Our hands were resting lightly on the mystic wand when it took off with a strength that had us each accusing the other of cheating.

"I'm barely touching it," I said as it made a fast circle around the edges of the board.

"Me either," my brother assured me.

"Maybe it's the baby."

We let the mystic wand go where it seemed destined to go, and a friend wrote the letters indicated with each brief pause of the pointer. When we asked the spirit to identify itself, the wand spelled "Daddy." The messages our friend transcribed were amazingly clear. "Take care of your mother." Then a string of vowels followed by, "Be a preacher. Make me proud." Dale was then in a graduate program at the Claremont School of Theology, in the process of deciding that a minister's life was not for him.

When we asked "Daddy" where he was, the pointer spelled out, "Band of angels, waiting for your mother."

We asked him how he liked it.

"I do not," was spelled out quickly.

"Why not?" Dale asked. Again the letters come quickly.

"Too many coloreds."

We shoved the board aside and sat staring at each other.

"Sounded just like him," Dale said.

"Exactly."

"Wouldn't you think that passing over to another life would bring enlightenment?" Dale asked.

"Eternity's probably not long enough," I said.

I stashed the Ouija board under the girls' games of Candyland and Uncle Wiggly in the back hall closet. Life with my father had been difficult enough when he was alive—why would I want to communicate with him after his death? I was free of him, of his drunken, stumbling gait, of the worry that he would set the house on fire with one of his forgotten cigarettes. It was over, the attempts to get him to quit, the false hopes dashed by the next drink, the emergency trips to the hospital. Thank God it was over.

*   *   *

It was not until four years after the Ouija board experience, my daughters were in their teens and my son was three, that my father forced his way into a dream of mine. He was dressed in a long white robe, and was surrounded by a glowing, golden aura. It was an embarrassment to me, when I awoke, to realize that my unconscious mind was so completely cliché ridden. In the dream, he did not speak, but seemed sober and alert. It was one of those strikingly luminous dreams, but I did not dwell on it. On awakening, I showered and dressed, whisked the kids off to school, rushed to the high school where I taught English, and immersed myself in the details of the day. My father kept his peace for another decade or so.

Then, late in 1982, as I was driving south on Highway 99, he invaded my solitude. I was on my way home from visiting Dale in Sacramento, and perhaps something was said, or remembered, that left a narrow opening for my father's unwelcome presence.

He probably got in while I was listening to Willie Nelson sing verse after verse of "Precious Memories." I suppose it was the verse about the precious father and the loving mother who reach out, in memory, across the lonely years.

Though I would never have described my father as "precious," I guess he *was* once precious to me. As a child I sometimes hoped that he and my mother would divorce, and I could live just with him. I thought he was more fun, and I knew he would never be so harsh as to ask me to pick up my clothes, or carry a dish to the sink.

On this day in 1982, he sat in the passenger seat, next to me, as I drove homeward. I tried not to notice, to think instead of the papers I had waiting to be graded when I got home, of how I would handle certain troublesome situations in my high school classroom, of my husband and three children waiting for me in Altadena. But my father somehow, sixteen years after I thought it was over, conquered my resistance. The scent of Yardley's aftershave filled the car, conjuring a memory of the bristle brush he used for lathering his face. He was humming, "Shall we gather at the river, the beautiful the beautiful river," in his soft tenor voice.

Every morning of his life, at least in my observation of it, he hummed the Baptist hymns of his childhood upbringing while he shaved. And then, once the danger of cutting himself was over, he added the words. "Shall we gather at the river, where the saints of God have trod," or "Blessed assurance, Jesus is mine," or "Just as I am without one plea"—simple, redeeming love and sanctifying blood songs.

At three years old, or two, or one, I sat on the cold tile bathroom counter and watched and listened, soaping my face with his brush. At seven, or eight, or nine, I would sometimes lean against the doorjamb, taking comfort in the sights and sounds of the morning ritual. Often, though, I was still in bed, and gently wakened by the familiar humming.

At sixteen or seventeen, I would first be awakened by the awful coughing. And then I would hear the water running, and the humming, and then the singing. Later still, when I and my two young daughters stayed awhile with my parents, after my divorce, I would be awakened first by the coughing, then the vomiting, and then, finally, the humming and singing. Always there was the humming and then the singing.

He had first appeared somewhere near Stockton, less than an hour out of Sacramento. He was in his thirties, with dark curly hair and brown teasing eyes. His short, stubby fingers were stained from years of holding Camels to the scorching end. His shoes were greasy, with sawdust clinging to them, as if he'd just walked out from behind the counter of his meat market. I heard his surprisingly familiar laugh, and then, suddenly, he was fifty-eight and near death. His eyes were dull and yellowed, his skin sallow, and he'd suffered so much loss to various nerve endings and brain functions that he no longer had the coordination to walk on his own or drive a car. He was begging me for someone, anyone, to get him something to drink.

On the morning of that clear, long-abiding memory, my father was scheduled to enter the hospital, against his will. When I arrived to join my mother and brother in carrying out the deed, he brightened.

"Here's my partner, she'll get it for me," he announces. He waves a five at me. "Go get me a half-pint, Shug, just enough so's I can quit shakin'. Then I'll quit. I promise."

"No. I'm not buying you any poison," I say.

He starts crying. "No one would bring my daddy anything when he asked for it either and he died. They let him die."

With those still fresh images brought to my consciousness, I turned the volume up, full blast, and tried to get my father out of my car. I stopped for gas in Merced. In the rest room I splashed my face again and again with cold water. Back in the car, I thought he was gone, but by the time I hit sixty the scent of Yardley's was again pervasive. He was singing "Amazing Grace."

I gave up. Sixteen years after his death, I gave up. It wasn't over. It had never been over. I granted his presence full recognition.

"God damn it, you really pissed me off, drinking yourself into the grave the way you did."

His eyes flashed at me—he who always tried to keep his friends from swearing in my presence, and who never took the Lord's name in vain.

"Watch that tongue, young lady," he says.

"Yeah, well, you did piss me off."

"Life was hard."

"That's no excuse for wasting it," I yell, feeling the long-buried anger erupt within me.

"Hard," he sighs, then turns silent. But he does *not* leave the car.

His was a hard life. A broken leg when he was twelve, set by a country doctor, by feel. A pinched nerve. Finally, after many weeks of constant, excruciating pain, his mother took him from their farm in southwest Arkansas to a hospital in Shreveport, Louisiana—over a hundred miles in a wagon pulled by two mules. The leg had to be broken again and reset. He became addicted to morphine. The injured leg ended up being one inch shorter than the other one, resulting in chronic back trouble which, in turn, offered an ongoing justification to drink.

It had been hard, too, for him to sell the meat market of his younger dreams. He'd opened the market in Temple City, California, in 1936. He worked six days a week, from seven in the morning to seven at night. He made his own sausage. He hand-picked his own beef at the packing house, filled any special order set for him, made personal deliveries, gave cooking advice, bordered the hamburger and sausage trays with fresh parsley. He wouldn't use a band saw on anything he cut for the case because the meat got fine specks of bone on it and didn't look as nice as when it was hand-cut. His hard work, good service, and attention to detail resulted in a successful business. For a while, in the words of his favorite poet, "life [was] good, and its tasks worth while."

I grew up as much at Dodson's Choice Meats as I did in the little, paid-for house on Cloverly Avenue. Near every birthday my father would wipe the grease from the meat hooks with an ammonia-soaked cloth, then lift me up so I could grab hold of the cool black, curved metal. While I hung there, like a side of beef, he adjusted the balance weights. Then he would lift me down and stand me against the wall, next to the walk-in refrigerator, and measure my height. This done, he wrote the date and my statistics on the wall, next to the telephone numbers of meat packers and fat renderers, apron launderers and bookies.

During those years my father enjoyed a prosperity beyond anything he had imagined when he proposed to my mother. Recently arrived in California off a failing farm and just learning the meat business, he had told her that if she married him, she would never have anything, but he would work hard and she would never go hungry.

After the war, with the advent of supermarkets, things went downhill for Dodson's Choice Meats. I remembered how hard it was for him to come to grips with the fact that the market he so loved would no longer make a living for him. When he sold it, long after it had ceased to thrive, I know he sold off a large chunk of himself.

"So, all right. Life was hard," I told the yellowed old man with the broken blood vessels lining his nose. "But I lost respect for you."

"There was always food on the table and a roof over *your* head," he said.

I could see the Sunday table as clearly as I could see the road ahead. It was laden with roast beef, potatoes, carrots, individual salad plates each with two canned pears on a lettuce leaf, garnished with mayonnaise and a few shreds of tilamook cheese. It was early afternoon and we, the four of us, were sitting at the dining room table. Maybe I was thirteen. In this particular "precious home scene," my father and I are, as usual, arguing. My mother, who has had enough to drink that she is feeling melancholy, is trying to distract us by passing the potatoes and telling us to finish them up. Four-year-old Dale, in a foreshadowing of his later vegetarianism, is feeding his roast beef to the dog.

My father is telling me his now worn-out story that in Arkansas the coloreds were happy picking cotton because they always had someone to watch out for them. I no longer believe he is allknowing. I ask him how he would like that kind of life. He tells me that's different, because he's white. He tells me that when I get older, I'll understand. That was his constant refrain, that when I got older I would better understand things and would come to agree with him. He infuriated me, but he did not bore me.

Coming into Delano, the Sunday scene jumped forward to evening, dining room table cleared, now covered by protective green felt pads. We were playing cutthroat pinochle. My mother was trying to make her bid. My father knew, after the first three plays, exactly how many trump cards she was holding and what they were. He led with a useless nine of clubs, forcing her to play her trump queen. She lost 350 points because of it. He and I laughed until tears rolled down our cheeks. She quit playing, complaining that we always ganged up on her.

I took my eyes from the road for a moment. He was still there, only now he looked as if he'd just got up from that Sunday afternoon card game. He was wearing a white shirt, with his tie loosened at the neck. He had on brown gabardine pants with a brown belt, and there was no sawdust on his shoes because it was Sunday. He was in his mid-forties—younger than I was at the time of the Sacramento to Altadena trip. He was laughing.

"We had some good times, didn't we, Shug?"

"Yes. But those last ten years—they were terrible."

"But we were partners, weren't we? You and me?"

I remembered another Sunday. Maybe on this Sunday I was fourteen or fifteen. Again we were arguing, but this time it was over whether or not he could climb the sycamore tree in front of our house. He bet me five dollars he could get up to the first branch, about twenty-five feet up the tree.

I took the bet. We walked outside. My mother followed us, telling my father not to be foolish, of course he couldn't climb that tree. He was forty-four years old, he had a bad back, and besides that, he was wearing his good clothes. While she was trying to talk sense to him, he was tromping through the ivy to the base of the tree. He stopped there and asked if I wanted to change my mind. I declined, and offered him the same opportunity. He responded by throwing his arms and legs around the tree and shinnying slowly, very slowly, upward.

Dale and I grew weak with laughter while my mother stood wringing her hands and telling him to come down. He continued his laborious shinnying. When he finally reached the first branch, I was struck by how far up he really was. We were all silent as we watched his eternal, awkward slide down the trunk to safety. He walked through the ivy, brushing bits of bark from his clothing. His shirt and pants were torn. His arms were scratched and bleeding. My mother was distraught. He was triumphant. I handed him five ones, baby-sitting money, hard earned at fifty cents an hour.

"We were partners," he repeated. "You can't deny that."

"You pissed me off."

"You probably haven't been a perfect mother," he said.

"No, but I haven't been blotto, either," I said, wondering if he knew that I, who had been a tee-totaler during his descent into cirrhosis, often had more than one glass of wine at dinnertime.

"I haven't abused my body to the point that I can barely walk, or digest food, or think straight," I told him.

He was old, and yellow, and bleary-eyed again.

"It's not good that you only think of me like this. What if your kids only remember the last ten years of *your* life? How will you like that?"

He was right. However the end of my life approaches, I want my grown-up babies to remember me reading to them, and crawling in bed with them when nightmares came, and kissing away their tears. I want them to remember me plunked down beside them in wet sand, building castles, and laughing with them at encroaching waves.

"Life was hard," he repeated. "The spirit was willing but the flesh was weak. . . . My life was more than those last ten years, though."

So finally, heading south on 99, sixteen years after my relief that things were over with him, I gave him what he came for. It was only fair. I let myself remember the good times. Staring over the grapevine, I looked to my right and saw the sallow-skinned figure fading. He was singing "There Is Power in the Blood." My throat tightened, and the tears I'd not yet shed for him gathered in my eyes. On that day I knew that no matter how pissed off, or hurt, or hardened I'd been, I could no longer lock my father out of my life.

Since that haunting trip from Sacramento to Altadena, I've let myself think of my father, refer to him, hear stories about him, without turning cold. He was a drinker and he ruined himself. But he was not *only* a drinker, nor was he only a ruined man.

The entire year I was fifty-eight, I kept comparing myself to my father at his dying age. He could barely walk with a cane, on a good day. His nerve endings were shot. He was left with very little muscle coordination. It was silly of me to liken myself at a healthy fifty-eight to the fifty-eight of my alcohol-ravaged father. But where it once seemed he died an old man, I began to see how pitifully short his life really was. And where I once was stubbornly angry with him that he wouldn't just say no, I now take a gentler view of his shortcomings. And as I've reflected on my own life, and how I came to be who I am, I can no longer deny his gifts to me.

* * *

The book of poetry I hold, trying to decide where its rightful place on my new shelves might be, is one of the few things I have that once belonged to him. It was first copyrighted in 1918. It looks good. On the cover, WHEN DAY IS DONE is embossed over a gilded scroll. EDGAR A. GUEST is embossed in gold. The back spine has title, author, publisher, all stamped in gold. The soft leather cover breathes a patina gained from pampering hands. But if a friend were to pick it up, read the singsong verse, the trite and sexist sentiment . . . Such a book on my shelf would be as much of an embarrassment to me as the unconscious white-robed, golden-auraed image I brought forth in that dream all those years ago. Having majored in English and taught high school English for twenty-six years, plus having a late-blooming career as a writer, I have certain standards. The literary quality of Edgar A. Guest does not meet my more high-minded standards. But those trite and maudlin verses had once been a door to a new world for me. And my father, who had been weak, and racist, and unable to love me nearly as much as he loved Early Times, had given me the key through which the Edgar A. Guest, and countless other, doors could be opened.

When Day Is Done pushes me back to September 1940, just after my fifth birthday, and my first day as a kindergartner at South Santa Anita School. I had been looking forward to school for a lifetime and on that day had experienced the biggest disappointment ever. Even bigger than the disappointment of not being able to keep the Banty chick my uncle Henry had given me the previous Easter. As soon as I got home from school that day, I rushed to the kitchen table, found the funnies in the *Los Angeles Times*, and was shocked to realize that I still couldn't read.

When my father came home from his meat market on the particular evening of my memory, he opened a cold bottle of Schlitz and poured some into my little cheese glass. He set the bottle in front of his place at the table, and the glass in front of my place. But instead of joining him right away, as was my custom, I stayed under the high-ovened stove, next to my dog, Brownie. My mother had told me I was silly to cry about not being able to read yet. She'd demanded that I stop crying, or she'd give me something to cry about. So I had retreated to my safe place under the high-ovened stove, and was comforting myself by petting Brownie's kind, silky head while he licked tears from my face.

"Come sit on my lap, Shug, and tell me about your day at school," my father invited, patting his leg.

I sat, looking at bits of sawdust stuck to a glob of grease on the sole of his shoe.

"Don't you want your beer?"

"You lied to me," I said, starting to cry again. "You tell me not to lie, but *you* lie to me."

His eyes flashed red as he grabbed me from under the oven and plunked me down in my chair in one swift move. He was a man who prided himself on his honesty, and did not take kindly to being called a liar by his five-year-old daughter.

"I can't read the newspaper," I sobbed. I reminded him of his promise that I would learn to read when I went to school.

Instead of demanding that I stop crying, he looked at me intently.

"Didn't they teach you anything today?" he asked incredulously.

"We played with big blocks and sang," I told him.

He shook his head, then turned his intent gaze toward my mother, who was peeling potatoes at the sink, her back turned to us.

"What kind of school is *that* anyway, Esther?" he asked. She did not respond to his question.

Again my father shook his head. Then he

picked up his Schlitz and walked into the living room.

"I'll teach you to read," he said, reaching for the thin black book of Edgar A. Guest poems. I grabbed my beer glass and followed him.

We started with the title poem, "When Day Is Done," and my father explained that letters stood for sounds. He read a few words and then helped me puzzle one out, and we went on that way, reading and drinking beer, until it was time for dinner.

A few months later the PTA sent out a bulletin on the pitfalls of parents attempting to help children learn to read. Different methods could lead to confusion, parents did not have special training, etc., but it was too late then. I had begun to make sense of the printed word, and no one could stop me. From the names of the Dionne quintuplets pictured in the bottom of my cereal bowl, to the signs for Morrell Ham and Kraft cheese on the walls of my father's market, to the Buster Brown insignia inside my shoes, every understood word was a mystery unraveled and a sign of my own emancipation.

"See? I wasn't all bad, was I?" he chuckles in my head.

I have to laugh, too, thinking of all the present-day turmoil over phonics versus whole-language approaches to the teaching of reading. Maybe the likes of my father should be traveling around with his ice chest of Schlitz, leading workshops for educators.

Besides teaching me to read, my father gave me a sense of narrative. On Sunday mornings I would crawl in bed with my parents, always getting in on his side. He would point out pictures in the rough plaster ceiling—pictures that at first I couldn't see but would become obvious to me as his story progressed.

"Look yonder at that old stubborn mule," he'd say, pointing overhead.

"Where?"

"In front of the boy. See that boy pushing at that mule's behind? Cain't get him to move for nothin'."

And then I'd see it. And the story would progress, digress, twist all over the whole ceiling.

"Ain't never even seen a mule, have you, Shug," he might say. "Esther, we got to take this baby home so's she can see a mule."

"We *are* home," I would remind him, but he would just shake his head and continue over by the old bossy cow in the corner of the ceiling.

My mother had told me, "Little girls are made of sugar and spice and everything nice, and little boys are made of snips and snails and puppy dog tails." But my father, when he came across a troublesome boy in a ceiling story, would tell me little boys were made of rags and tags and old cow bags.

"Now, Fay, don't tell her such things," my mother would say, sighing and getting out of bed to go start breakfast. Then my father and I would laugh the laugh of conspirators and continue on with a story that might not quite meet with my mother's approval.

For much of my life I've been a teacher, specializing in helping unmotivated students increase their reading skills and develop a love of reading. I am a writer. I work hard and am honest in my dealings with others. I speak my mind and I find much to laugh about. And, simplistic as it sounds, as I become more and more aware of the approaching end of my day, and the time when "the night slips down . . . I tell myself . . . that life is good and its tasks worth while." And for all of my father's great shortcomings, his gifts were also great.

Now, in this house that is not yet home, I use Murphy's Oil Soap to clean decades of dust from crevices in the eyelets of my bronzed baby shoes, the ones which have shown up after a long absence—buried under a pile of books. That's what my father does from time to time—shows himself after long absences. Today he has come through the books that have long sat unnoticed on out-of-the-way shelves, and I've not blocked his way. Another time he may come through the clicking of poker chips at a green felt-covered table, sneaking up on me when I'm calculating hole-card possibilities. I don't know when or through what trick he will show himself next. I only know he *will* come around again. It's not over.

I'm sixty-two, healthy and active. But if I neglect to rub lotion into my legs, even one day, my skin, especially around my ankles, becomes dry and flaky. It is sickly pale now that I avoid tanning because of the risk of skin cancer. It is my father's skin. It frightens me. What of my liver? But no, I don't loosen up with whiskey every morning, get a lift from it at noon, relax with it at dinner, and numb myself to sleep with it at night. And yet I am no foreigner to a failure of will—the consumption of fatty desserts, a constant neglect to floss, two martinis after the theater, skipping exercise morning after morning. I understand there is more to life than willing it right. He was weak and racist, and I've certainly not come to agree with him now that I'm older. But facing my own weaknesses, I can't rightfully judge his.

I have not forgotten the look of my father's

eyes, dulled with drink. I don't care to romanticize him into something he wasn't. But when a scent, or a song, or a quick laugh, sends him my way, I no longer resist. I let him linger. When it comes, I allow his memory to flood my soul, like the warmth of straight whiskey when it hits the bloodstream.

Father's Day

—∞∞∞—

J. A. Jance

J. A. Jance and her father, Norman Busk,
with the new Porsche Boxster.

FOREWORD

In the fall of 1947 in Marvin, South Dakota, my father, Norman Busk, was a thirty-four-year-old farmer with a wife and 3.2 kids. That year he spent six months bedridden with rheumatoid arthritis while my mother cared for the kids and the farm, hand-milking seventeen cows morning and night, walking to the barn when it was snowing so hard that she had to follow the clothesline to find her way back to the house. When my father finally consulted with a new doctor in Milbank, he was told that if he ever expected to regain his health, he would have to move to a high, dry climate.

Back home on the farm, my mother hauled out one of my father's old geography books. There, on a map of Arizona, they located the high desert town of Bisbee—a place where friends of theirs had moved several years earlier. Within weeks my folks packed us kids off to stay with an aunt and uncle while the two of them made a brief foray to Arizona to check things out. Which is how, a few months later, at the end of January 1948, after selling the farm, my parents packed their kids into the back of a Ford sedan. Pulling an overweight trailer loaded with all their worldly goods, they set off to make new lives in a new land—Arizona.

I once read an essay by Emmet Fox called "The Tenth Man." The essay talks about how in any given village in any given old country, if you went to where young people gathered on a summer's evening and listened to them talk, you would hear ten of them sitting around complaining about how constrained their futures were, how there was little they could hope for but to live in the same villages their families had always lived in doing the same things their forefathers had always done. At some point in the evening someone was bound to ask, why they didn't leave and go to America, the land of opportunity? If you returned to that same village twenty years later, nine of those people would still be there complaining. One of the ten would be missing— the one who had possessed the courage and perseverance to give up everything familiar and follow his dream. Fox maintains that America is a great nation because it is a country made up of those tenth men.

My father is a tenth man. The only difference is, the old country he left behind was the familiar open spaces—the rolling, grassy hills and lake-dotted lowlands—of America's upper Midwest. The South Dakota relatives could not have mourned more if he had taken his wife and children and moved across a roiling ocean. They stood rooted firmly in the South Dakota soil and sent us off with a carful of warnings and dire predictions: Arizona was so *far* away they would probably never see us again. Arizona was a *desert*. Arizona was *full* of snakes. It was *unbearably* hot there. The food would be so inedible that we were likely to *starve*. But my parents persevered, and off we went.

I was four years old, a carefree little kid who didn't worry that it was twenty-eight degrees below zero on the day we left the farm. I had no idea that the snow was so deep that my uncle had to hitch a team of horses to the car and trailer to haul them out to the snow-plowed county road. I have no recollection of the five days we spent snowbound in Enid, Oklahoma. My first memory is of the day we moved into the big old masonry house in Bisbee. It must have been late February or early March. What I remember most about that day is clinging to the ornamental iron fence that went all the way around the huge, fruit-tree-studded yard, staring up at the clear blue sky overhead, and feeling the warmth of the sun all over my body. That was what the move meant to me—adventure and sun.

But for my parents, and especially for my father, an invalid with a stay-at-home pregnant wife, the courage it took to make that move must have been daunting. My father got a job working underground in Bisbee's copper mines while his legs were still so frail that he had to pull his way up and down the ladders with his arms and hands. But the wise old doctor from Milbank proved to be right. The high, dry climate of the Arizona desert worked its wonder cure. My father regained his health and remains healthy to this day.

It's hard to write about my father without writing about my mother as well—they are a matched pair. They have been married for sixty-two years and live in a symbiotic kind of relationship where they know each other's punch lines and finish one another's sentences. To the outside world and to all of their seven kids, they have always presented a united front. There was never any point in trying to play one of them off against the other because what one said, the other backed to the hilt.

My mother was the disciplinarian in the family, the wielder of the immortal fly swatter. (In our house belts were devices for holding up pants rather than weapons of corporal punishment.) Nor was there ever a time when our mother said, "Just wait until your father gets home." If one of us required spanking, she was more than capable of doing the deed herself. Our father's major contribution was the threat, usually never carried out, of his "having to talk loud" or his having to use "the hard-handled knife."

Family meals in those days were eaten together. With seven kids, the logistics of serving such meals were fairly simple. Parents sat at either end of a long Formica-covered table. The three stair-step girls sat on one side, on chairs. The three stair-step boys, younger than the girls, perched on a long bench on the other side of the table. The baby of the family, the fourth girl, was in a high chair next to my mother. The silverware was a wedding present silver plate, and all but one of the knives had hollow handles. The one with a hard handle went to my father's place. That way, if one of the boys misbehaved, my father could, when called upon to do so, use the hard-handled knife to rap the boys on the tops of their little crew-cut noggins. I can tell you that the hard-handled knife was always where it belonged. So, although the threat was always there, it was seldom acted upon.

My father, Norman, was one of three brothers. Anyone who ever met my grandmother would have discovered that "Narmin," as she called him, the one in the middle, wasn't her favorite. Elmer, the youngest, who always struck me as somewhat effete, went off to World War II and came back "different" in some of the same ways some of the young men who went to Vietnam came back and still are "different." Elmer married a girl from the next farm and went off to live in Lead, South Dakota, where he worked in the gold mines and suffered terribly from the same kinds of rheumatism and arthritis that had once afflicted my father.

Harold, the eldest brother, was the sort of bachelor farmer that Garrison Keillor pokes good-humored fun at in his tales of Lake Wobegon. Harold was the "good" son. He stayed at home on the farm with both of his prickly parents, caring for first one and then the other, until they died. My grandmother was a demanding, self-centered shrew of a woman. Within two years of her death, Harold himself had a crippling stroke and was in a nursing home from that time until his own death several years later.

Which brings me to my father, the Prodigal. Family legend has it that "Narmin" was the black sheep of the family. Until my sainted mother, Evelyn Anderson, agreed to marry him, my father had a reputation for smoking, drinking, driving fast cars, and liking wild women. Once my mother agreed to marry him, however, he straightened up, flew right, and has been doing so for sixty-two years now.

My grandparents had a troubled marriage. For years while my father and his brothers were children, their parents didn't speak to one another. Instead, they wrote notes and communicated through their children. At the time my grandparents celebrated their fiftieth wedding anniversary with a great party at the grange hall in Marvin, South Dakota, it seemed to me that they should have had to deduct the ten years they didn't speak. I was in high school at the time, so it didn't strike me then, as it does now, how remarkable it is that, coming from such a troubled, dysfunctional home life, my father was able to go out and, at nineteen years of age, find the woman who was and is the love of his life.

My grandfather had a third-grade education. My grandmother had little more than that. It must have seemed to them that "Narmin" was terribly smart, and maybe that was part of the problem. He went off to college—one year at a normal school to earn a teaching certificate. While away at school, he wrote a short story for a literature class. My father called this classic tale of mistaken identity "The Chuckling Bandit." The teacher was so pleased with it that he wanted to submit it to a national literary magazine for possible publication, but my father wouldn't hear of it. The story was never published. Since the manuscript was not among the treasures that made the move from the farm in South Dakota to Arizona, I have never read it, but I'm sure that part of my father's frustrated-writer persona has found a voice in me.

My father isn't a man who has had a single career. His job history is a checkered one: teacher, farmer, county recorder, miner, carpenter, truck driver, contractor, life insurance salesman. From his example his children have learned that if one door closes, another opens. I don't believe any of us has ever been struck with abject terror at the idea of losing a particular job because we all know that, for someone unafraid of hard work, there will always be another job around the corner.

Television was long in coming to Bisbee, Arizona. On long winter evenings when a cold wind came howling down across the Divide, my father would read poetry to us from *The Treasury of the Familiar.* I especially remember him reading a poem entitled "The Wreck of the Hesperus."

It was the Schooner Hesperus
That sailed the wintery sea
And the captain had taken his little daughter
To keep him company.

For a middle child in a family of seven children, that seemed magical to me—to be an only child and so beloved that your father would take you along with him on an adventure like that, even if the voyage turned out badly in the end. The truth is, I liked and respected my father then, and still do. And my love of reading, which led inevitably to my love of writing, has its origins, I'm sure, in hearing those epic old poems filled with heroism and gallantry.

For a farm boy, my father was intrigued by some rather far-out ideas. Long before Eric von Danikin published his controversial books entitled *Worlds in Collision* and *Worlds in Upheaval,* my father got himself in trouble with the Lutheran church in Marvin, South Dakota, for telling the pastor that when Ezekiel saw a wheel way up in the middle of the air, it might have been filled with extraterrestrial beings who weren't exactly biblical in origin. In rural South Dakota in the twenties and thirties, it definitely wasn't okay to believe in the possibility of UFO's. My dad's interest in those kinds of possibilities led him into an informal study in comparative folklore. Upon finding a willing listener, my father can spend hours patiently explaining how all the world's cultures have their own peculiar versions of the Great Flood or the Day the Sun Stood Still.

My father is a man of honor, one whose word is his bond. He's never been a sheriff or a police officer, but he does have a great sense of humor. He's never met my character D. H. "Big Hank" Lathrop, but I think if the two men ever had a chance to sit down over a cup of coffee, they would naturally like one another. After all, they have a good deal in common—including their hero-worshiping daughters.

FATHER'S DAY

With a sigh Jennifer Ann Brady threw herself down on the living room floor and rested her head on Tigger, the panting half pit bull, half golden retriever that was Jenny's best buddy. Sadie, an older and far more reserved bluetick hound, lay resting a foot or so away. Jenny pulled the second dog closer so she could snuggle up between them. "I don't want to go back," she announced.

It was late Friday evening of what had been a scorching mid-June day in southeastern Arizona's Cochise County. In other years Sheriff Joanna Brady might well have been cleaning up dishes after a summer-style barbecue supper. But this year was not like other years. Andrew Roy Brady, a deputy sheriff and Joanna's husband of ten years' standing, had been gunned down and killed the previous September. Months into barbecue season, Joanna had yet to dust off and fire up Andy's trusty Weber grill. Rather than doing supper dishes, she was poring over the next year's budget figures for the Cochise County sheriff's department, trying to pare another $167,000 from a budget that was already bone thin.

Prior to her election to office, Joanna could not have dreamed how a never ending blizzard of paperwork would overwhelm her on a daily basis. She had always scoffed at people who had complained of having to bring work home. But now here she was, doing the same thing.

It took a second or two for Jenny's complaint to penetrate and register. "Don't want to go back to what?" Joanna asked.

"To Bible school."

Now it was Joanna's turn to sigh. "Look," she said. "We talked this over before you ever signed up. Marianne told us she needed an accurate head count. We agreed that if you signed up, you'd have to stay for the whole thing, that you wouldn't be able to drop out halfway through."

The Reverend Marianne Maculyea, pastor of Bisbee's Canyon First United Methodist Church, was not only Joanna's pastor, she was also the sheriff's best friend. Their friendship dated all the way back to junior high, and Joanna always tried to be careful not to presume on that relationship when it came time to keep or break church and Sunday school commitments.

"I know," Jenny grumbled. "But that was before I knew my teacher would be Jessica Shackleford."

Jessica was the college-age daughter of Marliss Shackleford, a local newspaper columnist who was forever using her gossip column, *Bisbee Buzzings*, to make Joanna's private life both as public and miserable as possible. At twenty Jessica was a junior at Arizona State University in Tempe. She had returned home to Bisbee for part of the summer and had volunteered to teach at Canyon Methodist's two-week session of Daily Vacation Bible School. As far as Joanna was concerned, the younger Shackleford sounded like a chip off the old block.

"What did she do now?" Joanna asked.

"She said I was obtuse," Jenny replied. "What does that mean? I tried looking it up. There was a bunch of stuff about angles that I didn't understand."

Frowning over her computer printouts, Joanna set the paperwork aside. "Whatever made her say that?"

"Mom," Jenny objected. "You can't do that, remember? You're not supposed to answer a question with a question."

Not answering with a question was one of the rules Joanna made her daughter live by. It seemed only fair to have the tables turned. "Obtuse is a ten-dollar word for saying not too bright," she replied. "Dense."

"In other words, stupid," Jenny supplied.

"Yes," Joanna agreed, "but you're anything but stupid, Jenny. Why would Jessica say such a thing?"

"Because of the Lord's Prayer."

"How can the Lord's Prayer make someone stupid?"

"We were talking about it," Jenny answered. " 'Our Father, who art in heaven.' Jessica asked the class who we thought the father was. I raised my hand and told her maybe He could be Daddy.

I mean, Daddy's a father, and he's in heaven now. Couldn't that make him a heavenly father? But Jessica said, 'No, Jenny. Don't be obtuse. The prayer's about God.' "

Joanna's first instinct was to go find Jessica Shackleford and give the girl a serious talking-to. Instead, Joanna thought long and hard before she opened her mouth. "That prayer is about what's in your heart," she told her daughter gently. "I think it's possible for it to be about more than one thing at the same time. And if you want to think about Daddy and about God at the same time when you're saying the Lord's Prayer, I think God is probably smart enough to sort it all out."

"You mean he's not obtuse."

Joanna smiled. "And neither are you." Thinking the conversation over, Joanna returned to her sheaf of paperwork. The biggest item in her budget was always salaries. Cochise County, which runs right along the Mexican border, is eighty miles long and eighty miles wide. Geography alone makes covering that much territory on a round-the-clock basis a complex undertaking. The added complications and profitability of international drug smuggling made Joanna's department's job that much worse. Her deputies were already working short-handed. Even so, the board of supervisors had just informed her that income was lower than projected and would require even more cuts.

"Then we had to make key chains," Jenny said.

Joanna didn't look up. "That's nice," she said.

"It isn't nice," Jenny continued. "They're leather key chains. For Father's Day. And I don't have a father." Turning away from Joanna, Jenny buried her face in Tigger's soft ruff and sobbed.

This time Joanna left the dining room table entirely. She hurried across the room, sat down cross-legged on the floor, and pulled Jenny into her lap. For several long minutes Joanna held the weeping child and rocked back and forth. "Shhhh," she murmured. "It's all right."

"It isn't all right," Jenny wailed. "I hate Father's Day. I *hate* it."

For an instant time melted away. Joanna Lathrop was fourteen years old and locked in nose-to-nose combat with her own mother. "It's a father-daughter banquet," she was saying to her widowed mother, Eleanor Lathrop. "I don't have a father, and I won't go!"

Two months earlier, while bringing Joanna and some of her fellow Girl Scouts back home after a weekend camp-out in the Chiricahua National Monument, D. H. "Big Hank" Lathrop, Joanna's father, had stopped along a deserted highway to help a woman whose carload of kids had been stranded by a flat tire. Putting on the emergency brake, Big Hank had stepped out of his vehicle to go fix the tire. After closing the door, he had stuck his head back in the through the open driver's window. "You girls stay put," he had ordered.

Those words, spoken to Joanna and her three friends, were the last ones Joanna ever heard him say. Minutes later, while Sheriff D. H. Lathrop struggled with the woman's jack, he was hit from behind by a speeding drunken driver—hit and killed instantly. Weeks and months afterward, those four words haunted his grieving daughter's dreams. "You girls stay put," he said over and over. "You girls stay put."

Three months after D. H. Lathrop's funeral, his uncompromising widow had insisted that Joanna attend her troop's annual Father and Daughter banquet. "It never pays to take the easy way out," Eleanor said in reply to Joanna's objection to attending the banquet solo. "It's a troop activity and you should be there regardless."

Sitting there on the floor, rocking Jenny back and forth, Joanna recognized that she had once walked in her daughter's moccasins. She, too, had despised Father's Day. For years it had seemed that every holiday did nothing but bring the pain of her father's loss back into focus.

"I know how you feel," Joanna said quietly. "It happened to me, too."

"It did?" Jenny asked tearfully. "Really?"

"Really," Joanna nodded. "I hated Father's Day for years. But the first big problem for me was the annual Girl Scouts' Father and Daughter banquet. I didn't want to go, but Grandma insisted. She said I *had* to go. When it came time for the dinner, she took me over to the high school and dropped me off."

Jenny sniffed and wiped her eyes. "What happened?"

"The banquet was held in the high school cafeteria. She stayed in the parking lot and watched me walk as far as the cafeteria door, but as soon as she drove away, I kept right on walking. I went on around to the back of the cafeteria, past the loading dock, and right on out the gate. I should have gone straight home, but I didn't want to face my mother. It was cold that night—cold and rainy. Even though I wasn't dressed to be out in the weather, I walked for hours. I was soaking wet when I finally went home. Afterward, I caught a bad cold that turned into pneumonia. I was sick all during Christmas vacation."

"I'll bet Grandma said it served you right."

"Exactly," Joanna said with a laugh. Jenny too smiled a tiny smile.

"But in a way, Jenny, Grandma was right. Just because we're sad right now doesn't mean that the world is going to stop for everyone else. Father's Day and Christmases and birthdays are going to come and go, and you and I have to keep on living each day. Eventually, you'll find that those holidays don't hurt quite as much as they did at first. At least that's what happened to me after my father died."

"You forget."

"No, you still remember. But it changes."

"Do you still remember how Grandpa Lathrop looked?" Jenny asked. "Sometimes, when I think about Daddy, I forget his face. I can't remember what it was like."

Joanna hugged her blond, blue-eyed daughter closer. "All you have to do is go look in the mirror, sweetie," she said. "You look just like him."

"Really?"

"Really."

Jenny pushed herself upright. "What about Bible school, then?" she asked. "Do I have to go back?"

In raising her daughter, Joanna was doing her best to avoid some of the pitfalls and mistakes she felt her mother had made. "That's up to you," she said. "You decide."

Jenny extricated herself from her mother's

grasp. "Thanks, Mom," she said. "Right now I'm going to bed."

Long after Jenny disappeared into the bedroom, Joanna remained on the floor, lost in thought. Eight months after Andy's execution-style shooting on High Lonesome Road, his loss remained the focal point of Joanna's life. At the time of his death, Andrew Roy Brady had been a deputy who was running for the office of sheriff. After his slaying some of his political supporters had urged Joanna to run in his stead. Eventually, she had not only agreed, she had also run and won despite the fact that she herself had never been a police officer.

Joanna Brady's husband had been a long-term deputy. Her father, D. H. Lathrop, had served two and a half terms as sheriff. Until her successful election to sheriff, Joanna's knowledge of the job had been strictly secondhand. Over the months it had taken tremendous concentration and effort on Joanna's part to rise to the challenge. But always, lingering in the background and never far beneath the surface, was the pain of Andy's death.

And today's painful mother/daughter discussion had made Joanna aware that the same was true for Jenny. On the surface she seemed to be a well-adjusted and easygoing if solitary child. She

loved nothing more than taking long late-after-
noon rides on Kiddo, her newly acquired sorrel
gelding. Accompanied by the two dogs, Sadie
and Tigger, Jenny would spend the cool early
evening hours exploring the far reaches of High
Lonesome Ranch. Girl, horse, dogs, and wide-
open spaces. This might have been a recipe for an
idyllic existence had it not been that Andy was
dead and his daughter worried about forgetting
his face.

With a sigh Joanna unfolded her legs and
tried to stand up. Sitting cross-legged had cut
off the circulation to one of her feet. With her
foot asleep and with pins and needles setting
fire to her lower leg, Joanna staggered back to
the table and resumed her work with the mass
of computer printouts littering her table. For another hour or so she struggled with the budget
before she finally gave up and went to bed herself. To bed, but not to sleep.

Hours after she crawled into bed, she lay
awake thinking about her own father, cataloging
everything she remembered about D. H. Lathrop. Like the hot cereal he often made for week-
day breakfasts—oatmeal, Malt-o-Meal, Cream of
Wheat, Zoom. There had been one flavor of cereal that was her father's own special inven-
tion—Whet-Meal, he had called it. That one had

come into existence through the happy combination of Cream of Wheat and Malt-o-Meal, and it had quickly become his daughter's favorite.

Breakfast had been the only time D. H. Lathrop had dared disturb the well-ordered neatness of Eleanor Lathrop's kitchen. The rest of the time the kitchen had been his wife's private preserve, and she had tolerated her husband's incursions into that domain with grudging ill grace.

With the benefit of adult hindsight, Joanna realized that those breakfasts had been symbolic of the dynamics at work in her family—she and her father versus her mother, Big Hank and Little Hank Lathrop versus Eleanor Matthews Lathrop, two against one. Over bowls of hot cereal, her father would wink and make jokes in the face of her mother's unsmiling disapproval. Where D.H. saw humor, Eleanor usually chose to see nothing at all funny.

Now, as an adult, Joanna had no doubt that Big Hank Lathrop had loved Eleanor—his Ellie, as he had called her—but a big part of his way of loving had been with a constant barrage of teasing. And Eleanor's way of loving had been grounded in thin-lipped criticism.

She had spent a lifetime trying unsuccessfully to "fix" her husband, everything from Big Hank's "Okie grammar" to his "backwoods table manners." In Joanna's charitable memory, her father hadn't needed fixing. He had seemed content enough while working underground in Bisbee's copper mines. Eleanor, however, had nagged and cajoled, wanting him to "better" himself. When, at her urging, he had left the mines to go into law enforcement, Eleanor hadn't approved of that either. "Being a sheriff is just another excuse to drive fast cars," she had sniffed disdainfully.

Sheriff Joanna Brady now understood how much that wasn't true. During her father's years in office, he, too, must have struggled with mounds of paperwork. Law enforcement administration, then as now, couldn't have included nearly as many high-speed chases and shoot-outs as it did bureaucratic showdowns with the board of supervisors.

And how was it that Big Hank Lathrop's daughter was now sheriff? The easy answer was that Joanna had agreed to run for office due solely to Andy's death. But was it really that simple, or were Joanna's reasons more complicated than that? How much of her becoming sheriff lay in a daughter's uncompromising hero worship of her father? And how much of it had to do with her mother's equally unwavering disapproval? Maybe being sheriff wasn't something Joanna Lathrop Brady had always wanted to do, but it was a way of keeping family traditions and feuds alive.

Which brought Joanna back to Jenny—to Jenny and *her* missing father. Like Joanna, would Jenny want to follow in her father's footsteps, or would she rebel against him? She had been an eager student of Andy's lessons in self-defense, just as Joanna had reveled in those early morning jaunts when D. H. Lathrop had taken her out to the rifle range for target shooting. Jenny had quickly mastered Andrew Roy Brady's secret thumb hold, and she had used it more than once to subdue schoolyard bullies several years her senior. D. H. Lathrop had insisted that his daughter learn to play poker. Andrew Roy Brady had taught his daughter to ride horses. No doubt Jennifer Ann Brady's future would be a compilation of what she had internalized from the two important but missing fathers in her life.

At some point Joanna fell asleep. The dream came later. Two men were seated at the breakfast nook of High Lonesome Ranch. Their faces were obscured, the way "true crime" television shows disrupt the facial features of suspects to conceal their identity. Beside one of the faceless men sat Andy's signature Stetson. The other man, sitting with one leg tucked under the other, stirred spoonful after spoonful of sugar into his coffee.

That was something else Eleanor had never been able to cure D. H. Lathrop of—his love for sugar.

Even though the two men had never met in life, they were together and talking in Joanna's dream, their two familiar voices flowing pleasantly back and forth. The problem was, Joanna couldn't make out any of their words. They were sitting there speaking, but she couldn't understand them. Joanna heard the low rumble of their familiar voices, but the words might have been in French or Greek or Chinese for all Joanna could understand them.

She had a sense that what they were saying was terribly important, as though between them they shared the secrets of the universe—secrets that were closed to Joanna. "Tell me," she begged. "I want to hear too."

But it was no use. Joanna awoke with a start and found her pillow wet with tears and the sun just lighting the sky outside her bedroom window. Her first thought on waking was the realization that she, like Jenny, was forgetting those two well-loved faces.

Almost without thinking, she flew to her closet. Standing on a chair, she dragged a big square hat box down from the topmost shelf. Carrying the box into the dining room, she cleared off her budget work and turned the box upside down on the table. A flood of family snapshots fluttered across the table. Leaving the pictures where they fell, she went to the kitchen and started a pot of coffee. Then, before returning to the dining room, she went to the laundry room and collected the stack of three-ring binders with plastic pages for inserting photos that Eleanor Lathrop had given her daughter for Christmas the year before.

"You're going to need to sort out all those pictures, label them, and get them in some kind of order," Eleanor Lathrop had said. "Otherwise, Jenny won't have any idea what some of them are."

Once Christmas was over, Joanna had put the binders away and out of sight, and not because she disagreed with her mother, either. For a change, she didn't. But right then, with Andy's death still so fresh, Joanna hadn't been up to the task. She hadn't been able to bring herself to face all those painful memories. Now she knew she had to.

Standing over the mound of photos, Joanna reached in and pulled out one at random. The pang she felt when she looked at it almost took her breath away. Andy, grinning, sat astride a horse, a pinto, with Jenny, little more than a toddler, perched between him and the saddle horn. Joanna remembered the sunny April day as if it were yesterday. The whole family had driven over to Willcox to visit one of Andy's friends, a fellow deputy who still lived at home on his parents' ranch. After lunch Andy had taken Jenny for a horseback ride. From that moment on, Jennifer Ann Brady had been bitten by the horse bug.

The next picture was one of Andy and Joanna standing side by side on the steps of Canyon United Methodist Church. Jenny, a sleeping newborn, was cradled in the crook of her father's arm. That was the morning they had taken their daughter to be baptized.

One after another, Joanna picked up the pictures and examined them. Having once survived the shock of seeing Andy's face again, it became easier somehow. There were holiday pictures: Andy and Jenny putting up the Christmas tree. Joanna carrying a platter laden with a Thanksgiving turkey. Joanna's favorite was one of Andy, his father, Jim Bob Brady, and Jenny all frowning in uniform concentration while they colored Easter eggs. There were pictures of Joanna and Andy alone and pictures of the whole family together. Working carefully and quickly, Joanna sorted the pictures into two separate stacks—into the photos she would give Jenny in one of the binders and the ones she would save until later.

Reaching deep into the pile, Joanna drew out yet another picture. When she held that one up to look at it, at first she thought it was a picture of herself and Big Hank Lathrop. But this wasn't one of the old-fashioned black-and-whites D. H. Lathrop had favored during Joanna's childhood. No, this was an unfaded color photo, one that was far too new to have been taken prior to Big Hank's death.

Holding the picture closer, Joanna realized her mistake. The girl in the photo wasn't Joanna Lathrop Brady at all. It was Jenny—her daughter. And the man—the one Joanna had mistaken for Big Hank Lathrop—was Bob Brundage, Joanna's brother. Born out of wedlock, he had been given up for adoption long before D. H. Lathrop and Eleanor Matthews finally married and had their second child, Joanna.

This dirty family secret, whose existence Joanna had never suspected, had lasted for more than thirty years, until long after D. H. Lathrop's death and after the deaths of Bob Brundage's adoptive parents as well. Then and only then had he come searching for his birth mother. He had entered Joanna's life only months before when he had shown up in Peoria as Eleanor's surprise guest at a family Thanksgiving.

Joanna had been floored. It was bad enough

that she'd had no advance warning that a long-lost brother even existed. Worse, she had endured years of criticism from Eleanor due to the fact that Joanna had been two months pregnant with Jenny at the time of her somewhat hasty marriage to Andy.

Ever since Thanksgiving, Joanna had seethed with resentment directed at both her mother and father. Her mother was a hypocrite and her father . . . He had lied to her as well by not telling . . .

Suddenly Joanna's knees went weak beneath her, and she eased herself into a chair. The pivotal conversation came back to her across twenty intervening years as clearly as if it had been yesterday.

"You've got no business taking that child to the rifle range!" Eleanor had raged. "She's a girl. There's no earthly reason for her to shoot."

"If my son were here, I'd be teaching him to shoot," Big Hank Lathrop had replied. "Since Little Hank's all I've got, I'm teaching her."

Joanna had heard that brief but heated exchange and had put her own childish spin on it. She had assumed it meant that her father had wanted a son instead of a daughter. Now Joanna realized Big Hank Lathrop already had his son, even if that child was lost to him. D. H. Lathrop had told his daughter the secret, after all; she just hadn't been smart enough to understand.

"Mom?" Jenny's sleepy voice floated into Joanna's consciousness. "What are you doing?"

"Sorting pictures."

"Why?"

"I'm getting ready for Father's Day," she said. "Once we have all the pictures in the books, we'll be able to see our fathers' faces again, yours and mine. That way we won't ever forget. See? Here's a stack for you, and there's one of the photo binders Grandma Lathrop gave us for Christmas last year. Do you want to put the pictures in the plastic sleeves, or do you want me to do it?"

"I can do it," Jenny said. "I'm not a baby, you know."

With time off for breakfast and lunch, Joanna and Jenny worked on the project until two o'clock in the afternoon. They ran out of binders and plastic sleeves long before they ran out of pictures, so some of the photos had to go back into the box, unsorted but not unstudied. As Joanna cleared away the remaining photos and prepared to return the hat box to its designated spot on the closet shelf, Jenny disappeared into her bedroom. She returned a few minutes later, holding something behind her back.

"Close your eyes and hold out your hands," she ordered.

As soon as Joanna did what she'd been told, Jenny placed a small object in her mother's up-turned palm. Joanna opened her eyes to find herself staring down at a leather key chain. The word DAD had been carefully burned into the burnished brown leather.

"I'm going to call this my Father's Day album," Jenny explained. "I want to put this inside along with all the pictures. Would that be all right?"

Not trusting herself to speak, Joanna could only nod. She looked on while Jenny struggled to unlock the rings of the binder. When the rings snapped open at last, Jenny placed the metal part of the chain over the topmost ring. Then she snapped the binder closed again, leaving the Father's Day key chain tucked safely inside.

"What do you think?" Jenny asked, looking up at her mother's face.

Tears stung Joanna's eyes. She had to blink several times in order to hold them back. "It's perfect, sweetie," she said. "For a Father's Day present, it's absolutely perfect."

Shadows of My Father

———⚬⚬⚬———

Carole Nelson Douglas

*Carole Nelson Douglas with her father,
Arnold Nelson, in Washington state.*

Strangers and relatives would call me a father-less child.

Country singer and coal-miner's daughter Loretta Lynn might call me a salmon fisherman's daughter, making my way in the world catching words with metaphorical nets.

Sociologists (I was a "latchkey child" before the phrase was coined to describe kids like me) would categorize me as a girl child who lost a father early in life, and was therefore likely to become a "high achiever." Sociologists love words like *therefore*.

Why are such girl children high achievers? Because lacking a father who harbors traditional (and limited) expectations of girls frees them to be all that they can be? Or because an unconscious search for a father figure makes them strive to be worthy of attention? Leave it to the sociologists.

My father was a Norwegian immigrant named Arnold Nielsen before the immigration process Anglicized his last name to "Nelson."

I thank that now politically incorrect process whenever someone asks if my pen name is "real" or was picked. It was partly picked . . . by an immigration official.

As I heard the story from my mother, who had an artistic bent, my parents chose Carole Nelson because the repeated *o*, *l*, and *e* looked well together. They had no notion that this name might ever appear on a book. I was particularly pleased when my second novel, and the first to sell to a foreign land, a seafaring seventeenth-century-set female swashbuckler called *Fair Wind, Fiery Star*, was sold to . . . Norway.

My father had immigrated to Canada with a wife who died in childbirth in the new land. He sailed back to Norway, leaving the infant son for his grandparents to rear, then returned to Canada. Eventually, he found his way to Washington state, where he met and married my mother, Agnes Lovcik, an almost-forty schoolteacher. He was over fifty when I was born, and didn't live to see my third birthday.

Memories of my father come in strobelike flashes. I have many vivid recollections before age three. My father is an elongated shadow.

Sometimes he stands before me, photographing me. Sometimes he stands behind me, pushing a yard swing. My most striking memory is one he'd probably not have wanted to leave me with:

I am sitting in the rear of a huge, humpbacked car like a black, shiny beetle. Beside me on the seat is a marvelous, magical, oblong black box with a small red porthole. If I turn the dial on the side, numbers race past the porthole. One, two, three, four, five . . . fascinating. Then my father arrives, a thunderous presence who discovers that I have exposed all the film for the family outing while left alone in the backseat with the Kodak.

I was seldom, if ever, spanked, that I know, but I never forgot causing that shock wave of adult exasperation.

I also remember the cats. My father the salmon fisherman attracted cats like Old Spice aftershave lotion later attracted women on TV ads. I can still see the multicolored, ridge-rimmed pottery nesting bowls he filled with fish, and neighborhood cats eating from them.

Those bowls, my memories, and an official refusal to let my father rest in peace followed me to Minnesota, where my widowed mother moved to be near two sisters. The first word I learned to spell in grade school was not "Dick," "Spot," or "Jane," but "deceased."

I used to fret, growing up in landlocked Minnesota, that a school official would someday descend on me as I filled out those annual, opening-day cards, and challenge my "deceased" father's occupation (the only parental occupation demanded), which I always, squirming, had to give as "salmon fisherman."

I was proud of my father's unusual occupation, but worried that I would be disbelieved. Everybody knew that salmon fishermen, and salmon, didn't live in Minnesota.

My father loved cats, my mother told me later, but she couldn't bear to have them in the house. "I would never be mean to a cat," she said, but she could never tolerate my having one as a pet. She allowed turtles, a parakeet, a duck, a rabbit, and finally a dog. Naturally all I ever wanted was a cat.

I was just like my father, she said. He had loved cats, and he had worked too hard. I mustn't work too hard. She was on me about that from my earliest school days. I had the intense concentration of the born myopic. I loved to draw and write. I made up poems lying on my back on the backyard hill, in Minnesota, watching clouds form and dissolve in the wild blue heavens above me. I thought everybody did that. I wrote plays I cast with neighborhood kids and stage-directed.

"Cats on My Back," an early effort, was about a mother who wouldn't let her daughter have cats until all the chores were done. When she did the dishes and finally did get a cat, the daughter threw it on her sleeping mother, who ran away screaming, "Cats on my back!"

To create a poster for the play (I was press agent as well as playwright and performer), I screwed up my courage to approach the nearby shoe-repair man, who kept a scrumptious Cat's Paw resoles cutout poster featuring a black cat in his store window. When he finally gave in and let me have it, I adapted it to fit my play.

Later, I attended high school and college with his only daughter, who became agonizingly ashamed of her Old World parents who talked with accents and kept a small house filled with froufrou. I adored them, although my own mother became suddenly embarrassing to me when I was a pre-teenager. She didn't talk with an accent or have froufrou, but she urged me to work less hard and to speak up for myself, which were the last things I wanted to do. I never learned to work less hard, but I finally learned to speak up.

You can't write about fathers, missing or not, without writing about mothers.

My father died because he worked too hard. I

learned that only when my mother died in 1983. Finally I understood why she had harped on my not working too hard, although I never understood why she hadn't liked cats. You can't really trust anyone who doesn't like cats. Even if she is your mother.

My mother died of a brain tumor. The hospice said that was a gift, because it was a beautiful death. At least it was swift, and my mother was the last to know of her condition, and the only one no longer able to understand it. But when it began creeping on—before I urged her to see a neurosurgeon during that Easter Sunday dinner when she described her symptoms and how her family doctor had brushed them off as "old age"—in those few months she began doing uncharacteristic things, that turned out to be her legacy to me.

As if having a presentiment of her coming death, she talked of writing down stories about my father's and her lives, and of me as a child. I encouraged her. Gave her blank-paged books that final Christmas. After she died, I found what she had managed to write down in a lined notebook. Two-and-a-half pages she had copied over, because her handwriting was becoming unreadable.

And it wasn't the whole story she told, but only

one indelible scene: how they had called her away from her grade-school classroom one day and told her my father had died on a salmon boat in the Pacific and that the body would come to port with the fish, on ice, some time later.

This shock had been the defining moment of her life, and death. From that moment on, I became an overprotected child. And incidentally, from that moment on, I became a catless as well as a fatherless child. Both facts were to shape me.

The story she jotted down was incomplete, frustrating. Salmon fishing is the world's most stressful job, rated even higher than firefighting. What makes these jobs perilous is long periods of inactivity interrupted by frenzied action: fighting a blaze, hauling a school of fish into a net. To the aging male constitution, this is the supreme challenge. My father on that fatal voyage had been illegally partnered with an underage boy, the captain's son. Who could protest the nepotism? Twice during the run of fish he felt chest pains and lay down. Twice he got up to play his part.

The third time he went down, he never got up again.

Because he was often gone on long voyages, his death was not the transforming loss it might have been. I do remember sitting on the 1940s floral forest and chartreuse green sofa, staring out the window, asking, "Why doesn't he come?" but I don't remember attending his funeral, and perhaps I didn't.

I have few mementos of my father: a Social Security card in brass, very few photographs of a man in a Sunday suit and fedora, a gold wedding ring so immense it seems forged for a heroic hand. An abiding love of cats and water, especially of the ocean.

My mother kept custody of all these material things and one immaterial thing more: guilt. My father had died an unconverted Lutheran, not a Catholic like her. He would never rejoin her in heaven. She had failed to convert him. Every Sunday when he was on land, she told me, he drove her and me to the Catholic church. He'd wait outside until the mass was done to take us home.

He was a good Lutheran, and I respect that. But in those days that was not good enough for a good Catholic, and my mother was haunted for the rest of her days by relatives who said she had failed to save his soul when she could, and so she had lost him forever.

To know my maternal grandfather, you had to know Pisek, North Dakota, a mere dust spot not named on most maps, fifty miles west of Grand Forks in the rich Red River Valley. A population of three hundred Roman Catholic Czechoslovakian farmer folk has dwindled today to a third of that. Many generations went from that valley, including my mother's.

Named for a town in Czechoslovakia (the other difficult word besides "deceased" I learned to spell early), Pisek was a milk-train stop on a grid of gravel roads bordered by grassy, damp culverts and flat farmland. Cars traveling those rutted roads left furrows of dust flumes like salt-flat racers without ever exceeding thirty miles an hour.

The house in Pisek, built at the nineteenth century's turn, fascinated in its stark simplicity. By the fifties the wide wooden porch that had served as a backdrop for family snapshots in the forties had been replaced by a small enclosed vestibule (shelter against the brutal winter winds and blizzards), a clumsy architectural afterthought seldom used, like an ugly hat that never suited its wearer.

So the back door was the real door, up a set of concrete steps with a pipe for a railing into a cramped entry room equipped with a washbasin, pitcher, and a pegged hat rack on which my grandfather always hung his straw summer fedoras.

The floors were vintage linoleum, and the

kitchen was a huge rectangle that housed a wood-burning stove and a silver-painted pump for water. Off this a small pantry had been converted to house a claw-footed bathtub. The facilities were seventy-five feet out back: the classic wooden shack that accumulated flies and rolls of toilet paper.

The house's first floor had been quartered: two large, two small rooms. The dining room with its long table and chairs enough to seat the entire family was decorated only by a bright gilt and green print of the Infant Jesus of Prague, a wizened child dressed in a stiff and ornate pyramid of costume as rich as a gold-foil paper doily. The two smaller front rooms, with their lace-curtained windows, contained the only furniture of interest, or at least of charm, to me, in the house: the golden oak secretary and huge rocking chair that was my grandfather's, and a golden oak wind-up Victrola that would play the John Whitman Big Band records still stored in its cupboard.

The front room hosted the crouching dark bulk of the furnace, and the mohair sofa on which I often slept as a child, under a small shelf added to the wall purely to support an old-fashioned ticking and chiming clock. The walls were painted with a lumpy cream enamel and bare except for wrought-iron outlines of a dancing Dutch couple one aunt and uncle had bought to hang above the sofa. In a corner near the furnace, a tiny wooden whatnot held a half dozen china figures, including an opalescent polar bear I still have today. There was little that was portable or nonfunctional in that house, but what I could find and bear away, I collected.

The upstairs space had been divided into big-windowed rooms with bare lightbulbs hanging from naked wires, few closets, stark metal-framed beds, an occasional dresser, and more sheer curtains, with no window shades.

We dressed and undressed in corners at night, aware that the houses in the town would be hard pressed to see us and that miles of lonesome prairie extended away behind the house.

My mother and many of her six siblings and their children visited Pisek every summer until the old folks at home died. I was the classic "are we there yet?" kid as we jolted that last fifty miles of choking gravel road from Grand Forks in Uncle Carl's port-holed early fifties Buick. North Dakota is flatter than a French crepe, a rolled-thin fieldscape broken only by the regular lines of trees planted as windbreaks.

Pisek announced itself with the white spire of its wooden church poking above the regimented treeline. Along with the grain elevators by the railroad track, the church spire was the town's loftiest landmark. The church may have been the community's spiritual center, but its literal centerpiece was a littered auto mechanic's yard. It boasted one former bank building *in memoriam* to the institution that had failed during the Depression, taking with it my Aunt Mary's trip-to-Europe money, a handful of beer parlors, and a general store. Then Jelinek's, the four-square brick store building, which once had been Lovcik Brothers, who were my grandfather W.F. and his brother.

So he had been a businessman-farmer, my grandfather, a more urbane sort who had occasionally traveled to "the Cities" (the Twin Cities of Minneapolis and St. Paul just under four hundred miles away), from which came carpeting and other major items for the simple town homes of the farmer folk.

In his early 1890s wedding portrait he is a sober, mustached young man. In my memory he is a slightly stooped, thin, slow-moving, mustached old man. And baby-sitter.

When I began kindergarten, my grandparents took the train from Pisek to St. Paul to spend the school year living with us. I shared a bedroom with my arthritis-afflicted grandmother. She cooked my simple soup-based lunches and filled the house with the after-school aroma of fresh-baked breads and poppy seed rolls.

My grandfather was in charge of another kind of roll, the roll of Lifesaver candies he kept on the high ledge of the oak pillars between the living and dining rooms, which he would dole out to me one by one as treats. He also told me tall tales. I would come home to learn that while I had been at school, my dolls had escaped their baby buggy, gone down the basement to turn on the laundry tub faucets and flood the whole basement and . . .

His simple tales were old-fashioned and exotic enough to thrill a city kid: stories of farm dogs named Sport and Watch and Time. He drew pictures of horses and dogs, the usual suspects in a farm scenario. The drawings were primitive, but an artistic bent runs in the family's younger generations, including me.

He taught me to play checkers and gin rummy, and sometimes I actually used to beat him.

But mostly he told me stories, and I've come to believe that was a major influence on my believing from an early age that I could tell stories too. In eighth grade I had to write a paper on My Most Memorable Person, and I chose my grandfather. I was told that hurt my grandmother's feelings, but I had too many surrogate mothers, and few father figures.

I was a sophomore in high school when we made our last annual family reunion trip to Pisek, not long after I had packed all my beloved Nancy Drew mysteries in the car trunk to give to my best friend in Pisek, Camille. That trip to Pisek began with the usual arrival ritual: accompanying my grandfather to admire the garden plot he tended a ways behind the house. The farm had long since been leased to tenants, but he always had a garden, and a hoe, wherever he went.

My grandmother died that night. I woke to the usual hush of voices murmuring on the first floor in that quiet, stark two-story house, and sensed that something dire underlay the usual lazy drone I heard. I lay awake for a long time, not wanting to get up and face what I suspected I would.

The family decided that Grandpa would go to live with his youngest son, Gerald, in Yakima, Washington, where Aunt Verna was home all day, instead of to St. Paul, where we were all at work or at school during the day.

Letters soon reported that he was growing mentally confused, and then, sadly, paranoid. In November we journeyed to Pisek again, out of season, for another burial in the small graveyard beyond the white wooden church, I sinking my grown-up ceremonial heels into the cold sod in the face of a brutally strong and cold wind. I was sixteen and he had been ninety-two. In many ways he had been my best friend.

Poor Uncle Carl Ash! He was German, not Czech, and worked as a construction supervisor, often out-of-state, yet often idle during the un-workable icy winters of my school years. Domestically, he was the only man among a trio of amazingly know-better women who were judge, jury, and executioner on all matters of permission and disposition regarding me and anyone else's own good. I was the only child among them, and he often acted as my advocate, whether it was urging that I be allowed to taste the Christmas wine, or that I could have a toy judged too old or too dangerous for me by the Superior Court of Three.

My unmarried Aunt Nell moved from Uncle Carl's and Aunt Mary's tiny new two-bedroom home to join my mother and me in an older, roomier two-story stucco house three miles away. Uncle Carl and Aunt Mary were childless. I loved to visit them overnight because they had a shower and Aunt Mary had a jewelry box she would let me explore. Aunt Mary was the family beauty, looking like Mary Pickford in a 1920s portrait I have framed in my office. A grade-school teacher like my mother, she had a more citified sense of style in dress and furniture. I have her lace thirties wedding dress and a twenties embroidered suit she saved. She could be stern as in her frequent "pipe downs," but she was also the most likely one to champion my cause. Perhaps the remnants of her dashing youth ultimately inspired my vintage clothing and jewelry collection.

Aunt Nell acted and looked like a mouse, but was a religious lion, one of Balzac's "pious, controlling women," I later decided. Overscrupulous to the point of being advised by 1950s priests to ease up, she was an implacable morally superior force that censored my (and everybody else's) behavior. She confiscated my copy of *The Three Musketeers* because it was on the Index of the Catholic Church's banned books; she suspected the word *mistress* had something to do with it. I learned later, in Catholic school, that *Musketeers* had made the Index because it supposedly glamorized dueling.

My mother was a talented teacher with a gift for art, outgoing, with many friends, but hounded by worry, mostly about me, mostly because of Aunt Nell's relentless application of the Guilt Standard.

Against the three of them, my Uncle Carl and I

could barely move unquestioned. He died from emphysema at Easter during my senior year in high school. I realized afterward that he had been failing for some time. Certainly the Lucky Strikes I "gave" him for Christmas (the adults suggested and/or bought the presents) didn't help, but I wasn't sure that he wasn't also ready to escape the Rule of Three.

But thank heaven for kindly uncles. I remember bounding down the stairs to greet and cuddle with Uncle Carl. He drove us everywhere, and acquainted me with vistas beyond our insular neighborhood: he drove us to see the Miracle Mile, the Twin Cities' first strip shopping center that he said would be the wave of the future; to where a new bridge would go someday, making the land a good investment; to the airport to watch the planes take off; to North Dakota; on Sunday outings to the country; to the doctor when I whacked a butcher knife into my forefinger while building a cardboard doll house; to play rehearsal at St. Thomas Military Academy over snow-clogged streets in my senior year of high school.

He was there when I was given a toy pedal car that was immediately taken away. (Too big for me, or did the Triumvirate not approve?) My first bike was a behemoth with turn signals and a horn, and it really was much too big and heavy for me, rather like the 1958 Oldsmobile 88 my mother bought to learn how to drive with, so she could teach me to drive. The first time I took the bike around the block, I lost control on the turn by the corner grocery store where the sidewalk sloped down toward St. Clair Avenue. I jolted out over the unused streetcar tracks and could stop only in mid-intersection. Luckily, no cars were coming. I never told anyone, and so kept the bike.

Uncle Carl drove us to get my first puppy, a Pomeranian that proved too difficult for my working mother to housebreak and didn't last; later to adopt the adult Pomeranian that replaced it, and that did last: Bambi, a fox-faced little dog who waited for me in the window every day after school and who retreated to a chair, head on crossed paws, to pray the rosary every night.

In my later grade-school years the grandparents no longer came to stay the winter. I became a latchkey kid, coming home at noon to heat canned soup on the stove and listen to soap operas on the old wooden radio. Uncle Carl was often home alone also, and there to call on if something happened.

But as much as my grandfather, and later Uncle Carl, acted as my caretakers, I ultimately also acted as theirs.

My grandfather's job was to walk me the two blocks to Nativity Grade School on my first day of school each year. We were assigned to lines for our new classrooms. When I was in the second grade, my grandfather herded me into the wrong line. I knew it was wrong, but I stayed in it, ending up in the wrong classroom. When my name wasn't called, I was discovered and sent to the right classroom. Although it was humiliating to be misplaced on the first day of school, I didn't want to embarrass my grandfather. I already knew that he was old and could sometimes fail to get everything right. Pointing it out would hurt his dignity.

Most only children have to mature early.

When I was an eighth-grader, our neighbors across the street acquired a new dog, a German shepherd. I had "met" it with the family present. When I came to pick up one of the children for our customary walk to school, the dog, on a chain, was sitting in front of the house. It growled at me. I was taken aback, but I liked dogs and had never encountered a hostile one. I moved to pass it.

It leaped like Rin Tin Tin, its teeth tearing into my heavy wool winter coat. Luckily, instinct had made me throw my right arm up before my face and neck, because the dog went for my throat, again and again. I backed up, screaming, but no one heard. Luckily, the dog's chain ran out before I could be knocked down.

Despite my sturdy coat, my upper arm had several teeth wounds, so I called Uncle Carl to come take me to the doctor. He was reluctant, sure I didn't really need medical attention. (I now realize that the emphysema was at work, making him weaker and unwilling to stir.) I insisted. The bite was bad and I had to get medical attention, and a tetanus shot, right away. He came then, but I was growing into my own caretaker.

His death four years later, just before I graduated from high school, was a terrible blow. My grandmother, grandfather, Uncle Carl, and favorite Uncle Chris had all died within a two-year span. Yet Uncle Carl had a last legacy to leave me, though I wouldn't discover it for thirty years, and then in the fashion of melodrama.

By then the overbearing dynamics of my family of three mothers had been faced, faced down, and were winding into their last days. I returned to the old house on the death of my Aunt Nell in a bitter January 1992. Mary had died only the year before, in her nineties in a nursing home, after a slow descent into dementia beginning with my Uncle Carl's death thirty years earlier. My mother had died nine years before, with Nell living on in the house. As executor of Nell's estate, my job was to clear away the last remnants of that household, forty-three years of "home furnishings," which included clutter, and memory and unresolved conflict.

So I was cleaning out the house, including the stockpiles of support hose stuffed into every drawer, empty suitcase, and brown paper bag. The house of women was a stockpile of support hose.

When my Aunt Mary had died, her 1940s mahogany furniture hadn't sold. My mother couldn't bear seeing it discarded, so she had bought some pieces. My Aunt Mary's dressing table had sat in my former bedroom for years, under its elderly lace dresser cloth. The top center drawer was lined with old wallpaper. Being a thorough sort, and perhaps being a veteran of estate sale hunts, I lifted the wallpaper.

A document lay beneath. A long document, legal length, of several pages. It was my Uncle Carl's will. I read through it, fascinated by this thirty-some-year-old find.

And I learned that someone in my family besides my mother had been concerned for my survival. I was Uncle Carl's chief heir after his wife, Mary. It was as if my old ally in independence had reached from the grave to give me the approval that had been withheld by my Aunt Nell for so long.

Uncle Carl had the final word, after all.

Uncle Carl was not my only shadow father. I had the six most fascinating uncles on earth. So I thought. No doubt the fascination existed because the men in the family were an exotic species to me, reared as I was among women and teaching orders of nuns.

My husband, Sam Douglas, and I were both predominantly connected to the maternal side of our families. He was the oldest grandchild in his family and, as a child, had preferred the company of the women to that of the men. Men in that farm family liked to fish and hunt; Sam was to become a singer, actor, and artist, and preferred less destructive pursuits.

I was the youngest grandchild in my family, and I preferred the company of my uncles rather than sitting in the kitchen with the women, doing disgusting things to naked chickens.

What I most liked about hanging around the uncles was the fact that they really didn't do much, at least not in Pisek, which was where I mostly saw them. They sat and talked sports and politics. They congregated in the dark by parked cars, with one running so its radio could announce news from a presidential convention in a small, tinny voice.

They played mumblety-peg in the yard, a

game of skill involving throwing a jackknife from various positions, including at your opponent's feet. They let me play and never once mentioned anything about it being dangerous. I got pretty good at it, and still keep out an eye at estate sales for a good mumblety-peg knife, though none of them seem to be the proper size and heft that I remember.

They took me along for rides in the car to places the women didn't know they were taking me and I wasn't supposed to be: like waiting outside while they stopped at a local beer parlor, or in the backseat when my Uncle Al took my Uncle Chris's Oldsmobile 98 up to its maximum speed of one hundred twenty miles per hour on the paved road between Park River and Pisek.

It was my Uncle Chris who began teaching me to drive. He was my favorite uncle after Uncle Carl, a man early bent by World War I injuries and time in the trenches. A sixth-grade dropout who was homesteading as a teenager in Montana when he went into the war, he came out to spend six years in veterans hospitals while my Aunt Bunny (Angela) waited for him. They moved to New Mexico because the doctors said that was the only place he would survive.

Did he ever! He became the only well-to-do member of the family, but his only personal luxury was the Oldsmobile 98 he traded in every three years for a new one. Extremely shrewd, he was also a devout Catholic bent on good works. A young high school dropout who worked for him resisted the idea of taking the GED equivalency test, so Uncle Chris bet him that an old man with a sixth-grade education could outdo the young guy on the test. He didn't, quite, but the young man passed, and that was the result he wanted.

He scared me a little. He had two sons before he had a daughter; he would roughhouse by grabbing me and not letting go, and I couldn't get loose. "Challenge" was his middle name.

He used to let me steer the Oldsmobile over the gravel roads around Pisek when I was fourteen, keeping his foot on the gas. Once he suddenly grabbed the Oldsmobile's wheel, pointed the car down a steep, rutted path that made a deep hammock between two branches of the road, then left the wheel and gas pedal totally to me to get us out of there. I did.

He had played about every board game in history during his long hospitalization and could beat just about anybody at anything. We played Scrabble, and despite my precocious word grasp, he always beat me too.

Until one reunion, held at my Uncle Gerald's and Aunt Verna's house in Yakima now that my grandparents were dead, during the World's Fair in Seattle in '62.

We had our usual game of Scrabble and, for the first time, I won. I felt stunned, and terrible.

Uncle Chris lifted my arm above my head and paraded me through the house so everyone could see. "Champion!" he hailed me. "Champion." He was the ultimate good loser, but I didn't feel like a champion. I felt as if I had lost something forever. Winning against Uncle Chris, while it had become, like all things long denied, something of a childhood obsession, was *wrong*.

Driving home from that reunion, my Aunt Bunny at the wheel of the Oldsmobile, something happened and the car ran into a ditch. It wasn't that serious an accident; she was all right. But Uncle Chris died, probably because the accident was too much for his war injuries.

I can't help thinking that some intimation of death looming on the horizon caused Uncle Chris's Scrabble loss. No one ever beat him but death.

And that made four shadow fathers gone, three in two years.

That's when I stopped finding shadow fathers, or looking for them, when the shadows grew so weak that they disappeared. But occasionally they would surface.

As a child, my first literary agent had escaped Russian pogroms against Jews. Like my father's family, hers had emigrated to Canada. She had uncles she never saw again. Later, as the widow of a publisher, she was too active to retire. She was not a young woman when she became my agent, and she wasn't a well woman toward the end of our eight-year association. An editor once remarked that she was "more like a mother than an agent." Certainly she could act in the stern model that I remembered. But late in our association, unknown to me, she began showing signs of senility. It was perhaps in such a state that she met me for dinner in Manhattan and had two instead of one drink before dinner, then related her sad yet ultimately triumphant family history, adding, "When I first met you, I said, 'This is not an ordinary American girl.' What are your antecedents?"

I knew what she meant. It was the "hard work" my mother warned me against, my father's seabound immigrant inheritance. Not pogrom but poverty and world war had driven him to the New World; perhaps some genetic inheritance had driven me to work hard, something besides my passion for self-expression and creativity. "You're just like your father," my hardworking mother would say. "You mustn't work too hard."

We are all immigrants, in this land and in this life, even Native Americans who crossed the icy land bridge from Siberia, and the spirit that drives us is both blood and beyond blood.

And that is the legacy my father finally gave to me: that we can't escape what we are, and that what we are is what we make ourselves. And that takes time and memory and hard work.

It's a paradox. We are indentured to our pasts, and our pasts make us free. I am the salmon fisherman's daughter, and something he never dreamed of, a writer on the waters, who scoops up words in a shining silver net, who brings concepts instead of scales to market.

It is still the same fight, to wrest a life and a living from the universe, to say we were here and leave daughters on the wave tops, singing. The mermaids and the cats have always sung for me, despite everything, and always will. And for that I must thank the many shadows of my father.

Ladder Work

⊸∞∞⊷

Noreen Ayres

Noreen Ayres and her father, Jerry Pahlka,
on the Texas lake behind their home.

She saw the lights coming from off the main road. "That's Turner already." He was fifteen minutes early. Dacey Ann had hardly got there, 4:20 by her watch. Certain people would say she was bird-dogging, trying to get the best spot first. Turner, though, was an honest man. He'd give her nothing ahead of the others.

The door of her add-on camper shut solidly; then the key went into her shorts pocket next to her knife and last two dollars. In her other pocket was a roll of adhesive tape for her fingers. She'd need this if she was going to pick fast and make up for the bad luck on the northern run.

Turner stepped out of his truck, looking her way. His hair wasn't any whiter, but he seemed to treat one leg more tender.

"What you got there, Turner? Another wino crew?" She eyed the two men in the truck bed and could tell they didn't know a word of English. Nationals. He must be expecting a lean crop. Otherwise, he'd be paying an American wage. It wasn't she begrudged a man a dollar, but she'd just come from a state where Indians underbid and all the Orientals had their dozen little kids in the rows by age five, and how the heck could you compete with that going on?

"Well, shoot a bug, if it ain't Dacey Ann Adams," Turner said. "In the flesh and a little less of it than when I seen you last." He came close and shook her hand, still could have broke it, she was aware.

"I shed about a hundred ninety-five," she said, "and twenty of it was mine." In the quiet her soft voice sounded like wind down a draw even to herself.

"You and Paul? Now, that's a damn shame. Paul's a nice guy."

Turner studied the ground, could have been sorting out just who Paul was, for all that. Dacey Ann used to get around a bit, with no absence of beaus. Each season saw a new one there for a while, or so it seemed, and if anyone thought she was embarrassed by it, they thought wrong.

"Paul's all right in a pinch," Dacey said, "but you have to pinch him a lot to make him see reality from a dream." Which wasn't exactly what she meant, but she'd said it and that was that.

"Well, now, we all got to have some vices or life ain't worth livin', now is it?" Turner said. He drew his notepad with the columns on it for accounting off the windshield, where he'd set it when he got out of the truck. "So. You're lookin' for a ladder."

"That I am," Dacey said. "Been rainin' all season up in the Yakima. Rain, then sun. Rain, then sun. Fruit's all busted. Down to Kennewick, too. They was flying 'copters over to dry off the trees, but it don't do no good. I don't know why Paul had this idea to head north first, bassackward, but that's Paul."

"I got a scrappy orchard here myself," Turner said. He tufted the dirt with his boot toe. "You coulda sent some o' them rain clouds my way."

"I'll think harder on it next time." The sky behind Turner's truck was brightening. Bugs were up already, their tiny silhouettes looping against the yellow skirt of the horizon. Down the road came a picker truck pulling God's own powder puff behind it. "*Has* been dry, looks like."

"Girl, I got a year-old duck don't know how to swim."

"Damn you, Turner. I come here feelin' sorry

for myself, and you got me near bleedin' over you before the sun's half rose."

Turner liked that reaction, brushing his nose to hide a grin. He set his notepad back and started speaking to the nationals, in their language. They clambered out of the truck bed with pails. Then he lowered the tailgate to unload stacks of wooden fruit boxes.

Dacey pitched in, lifting as many as Turner, easy. She was tall and strong and took satisfaction in the fact she was equal to any fruit tramp on the cherry run. Citrus, now, and apples, was another story, but not by much. As for row work, stoop labor, lanky doesn't do so well. Leave that for the Chinese. Their center of gravity's lower.

The picker truck stopped several yards behind and was emptied of three men and two women. Dacey watched as the five moved ahead like wraiths in a moon fog. She knew them, the family Garver, knew how deceiving were their looks: slight, smooth of muscle, and mild in features and speech. Breakfast at a pickers' camp, the family would hold church while the smell of potatoes and onions cloaked the air for fifty yards and hungry men's stomachs churned. Anyone could come to table, but they'd have to pay fifty cents and listen to a sermon almost till the Crisco cooled. This was the Garvers, but they had another side, too. Every single one, down to the women, had seen time. Each had their separate reasons, and you could debate it over a campfire till the crickets croaked, and no one would know the truth but the family Garver itself, and even then that wasn't a certainty.

"Hello, Dacey Ann," the youngest one said, shy of Dacey Ann's own birth year by one.

"Hello, LuEthel," Dacey said back. First rays struck LuEthel's hair and turned reddish tones pink. Her smile made up for a figure all bones and a face narrow and near devoid of cheekbones. She could wear a getup that was overalls made into shorts over a bathing suit, and no man would turn a head. LuEthel couldn't hold a baby inside her long enough to bear, but she kept trying. Last count Dacey remembered was eight. LuEthel's time in jail had something to do with medicine she had tried to get from a stolen prescription pad, nostrums she thought would keep a baby in a womb. Corliss bailed her out and then went to jail himself for siphoning gas out of an old man's Buick to get there.

"You're lookin' good," LuEthel said. Dacey nodded her thanks. "Braid's way longer."

Dacey was going to say something, but LuEthel's husband, Corliss, said, "Legs, too," and LuEthel gave him a look.

One of LuEthel's brothers, the one with an eye

that couldn't shut on its own so he had to patch it, said, "Lost you some weight. I liked you better before."

"Thanks, Herschel," Dacey said, then nodded to the others. "Vernon. Wright. Minnie Jean. Nice to see you all."

Minnie Jean, mother of the clan, smoked a cigarette that stuck up at a forty-five out of the corner of her mouth while she draped the pick-sack strap over her neck. She asked Turner how many pickers he figured on.

"I'm about full-handed now," he said, glancing at Dacey and the nationals.

"That's a sad thing, then," Minnie Jean said. "We met up with some'll be coming over. Makes you wonder what the Lord has in mind, weather like this."

Turner said, "I'll line you folks three drives thataway," and pointed west at the rows between the trees where the tractor had gone down. To Dacey he said, "I'll show you your set after I line out them other boys." He nodded toward the nationals, then walked their way.

LuEthel hung back while her family proceeded with boxes and ladders to where the trees still stitched dark against the growing light. "Dacey Ann, Mama says she saw Ernest last month down Fresno way."

"Saw who?"

"Your papa. Ernest Little. Mama says he's pickin' over at Marysville, gonna come to Stockton in a bit."

"Well, I guess he'll be comin' for nothin'."

"He asked after you. She told him we hain't seen you in a while."

Dacey Ann scrutinized the trees, then said, "I wonder if this whole thing is worth even settin' up a ladder for. Maybe I should go on down the road. Leave this pickin' for you. 'Course, y'all will be rough-pickin' and Turner will can you, every last one, before noon, and I wouldn't be wantin' to leave him short."

"We're not rough pickers, Dacey Ann."

Dacey went and looked in Turner's truck bed even though she knew it was empty, all the boxes unloaded by now.

LuEthel came up beside her and said, "I hope you was kiddin' on that, Dacey Ann."

"Don't take everything so serious, LuEthel," she said with a smile. " 'Course, I know you Baptists are spare on humor."

"That ain't true neither, Dacey Ann, or we wouldn't tolerate *you*. Besides, we ain't Baptists, we're nondenominationals, so we can fun on anyone. Better watch out or you might be next."

"Well," Dacey said, grabbing up her pick sack

where she had left it by the camper, and a pillow-case that held a quart mason jar of water, "let's us go earn us some money, what you say?"

"Aw, we got so much of that it's underfoot," LuEthel said, a smile sneaking at her mouth. Her Picker's Pal bucket dangled from her right arm, and her pick sack was draped over the other. "I got some jerk, you want it."

"I'll just take it, too, if it's from Grandma Garver."

LuEthel stopped, transferred her pick sack to the other arm, and reached inside her dress pocket for a flat of waxed paper. Dried meat was nestled next to fried bacon, and she gave two strips of each to Dacey. "Beer's in our camper. Herschel's stingy by it, but you can get you one while he's still scoutin' his fruit."

"I got water," she said. "Thanks again."

"Mama said Ernest is looking real good. Said he seems to be at peace."

"LuEthel," Dacey Ann said, stopping in their walk and looking at her directly, "I wouldn't take no more notice of that man than perfume on a pig. So let's just leave that subject be."

"Dacey Ann, you can be a pitiless girl."

"You know I can, LuEthel."

"I know another side, too, sister," LuEthel said. LuEthel looked like a little child, humble in her white socks and low-cut boots beneath that overall getup. Her hair curled out before her ears while the rest of it was tied back with a shoelace. With all that, Dacey Ann could let herself feel that pang for a moment for a sister.

But a sister circumstance was not to be. Heaven nor a flood of tears could change that. And a bunch of the reason for that condition was a man named Ernest Eugene.

"You got a heart, when you want to use it," LuEthel said again.

Dacey walked toward her set, saying, "Don't spread that lie around. I got enough trouble as it is."

A glance back caught LuEthel's smile and wave before she disappeared behind the trees.

Turner gave Dacey Ann four drives away from the others, and she was grateful for the gift of solitude. Solitude suited her nature. People, you could take 'em or leave 'em. Overall, it usually worked out best you leave 'em.

Ernest Eugene Little. Who was he to her? That old man. All his life, as useful as a screen door on a submarine.

He'd show up out of nowhere, dark hair lopping over his ears like nest feathers, his blue eyes wet with moonshine and his pawnshop guitar bouncing off the wiry muscles of his back. Mama would ignore him, then fight with him, then love him. She'd forgive him and forgive him, right up to the last.

And then one morning he'd be gone.

Just as Dacey Ann had almost lost her shyness around him, he'd be gone. Just as she'd re-memorize his features, or be able to single his voice out in a crowd, or have the words to "Hey, Good-lookin'" down right so she could surprise him while he gee-tar picked that tune after dinner—he'd be gone.

Once, a tent neighbor said of her daddy, "He ain't married, but his wife is." The man laughed and said he wished the same for himself but was too much a coward for it, his own wife loaded with bullwhip and mean dog. Dacey Ann had been eight years of age then, and she'd had to mull it over a bunch of times before she came to understand.

And that wasn't the half of what Ernest Little left in his wake years down the road, but that was the first, and the middle was just more nonsense and needles, if you let it get to you. And then that last. That sledgehammer. The one you couldn't get over. . . . What did LuEthel know? Go pick your cherries, LuEthel, Dacey Ann said to herself, I'll take care of my own.

*   *   *

Her ladder set firm to the earth, Dacey mounted, brushing aside a web wet with dew and weighted with a spider. Its long blond legs flexed and bothered, and she watched with some regret its struggle to find new purchase. Its brother lay up ahead in her path, and this one she just mashed against a broad limb with the back of her bucket before she set it on the pail rest. Held at the back by the same strap looped around her neck, the sack gaped in front like a frog's mouth run forever stiff with whalebone. She'd fill the bucket first, then the sack.

Curling her unwrapped fingers around some deep red clusters, resilient bubbles in her palm, she tugged the cherries free and dropped them into the pail and could hear in the morning quiet the two nationals pitching their discoveries against the aluminum as well, the sound a soft xylophone.

"Found you a cotton field, Dacey Ann?"

"Yes, sir, I did," she said, answering the voice below. She saw him set boxes on the ground. "By the way, Turner, what you payin'? I forgot to ask."

"Why, I'm payin' what you're worth, Dacey Ann."

"Well, hell, Turner. It wasn't my idea to work for free."

She heard him laugh at the old joke, then saw the top of his straw hat move away beneath the limbs. Now, why couldn't she have had a daddy like that, steady, smart, and honest? Paul, her husband, always said she had to get over her grudges, and Dacey Ann would just argue back, Why?, a grudge is more solid than a traveling lie. Because I care about you, is what he'd say then, and Dacey Ann still didn't get what the big problem was all about.

The sun was full up now. Soon the last of the scent of evaporating irrigation water would be gone, replaced by currents of insecticides and raw dust and small field carcasses rotting in the furrows.

Over the treetops birds were scrapping with each other, and in the distance the call of a train channeled across the flat land. That was one thing Dacey liked about being a fruit gypsy, early rising, to see the beginnings of the world where humans trudge their rows like the ants they had to admit they were. Ladder work gave you a new perspective. Stoop picking, all you saw was dirt and a blaring white sky if you dared.

As a teen Dacey had told herself she'd never pick after she finished taking care of her mama. But after her mama died, it was like Dacey Ann just didn't know what else to do, and the life gets in you, and you can't stand the thought of the lack of open air, so she kept on.

Patterns of light marbled her legs and hands so she looked painted, and she liked the look of it and began to hum a song. She made a trip down the ladder to empty both bucket and sack, and when she remounted, it seemed to her ten degrees cooler than below. It wasn't she minded the heat all that much most times, but too many days of it too soon got you up to be grouchy, same as too many days of wet made you mad as a rooster under a rainspout. She could, if she was of a mind for it, grump to Turner that the trees weren't spaced far enough apart; the limbs tangled in on themselves. Clusters were hard to find, and when you did find them, you had to tug them through the limbs. That might cause you to bring spurs along, where the new cherries come from. Then nobody's happy.

But he wasn't the one who planted them, after all, and she'd been trying of late to learn how to keep her tongue. Didn't want to be, like Paul accused her of, all mouth and no brains. Hoof-in-mouth disease, is what he said she had sometimes. Comments like that would cause a cuss fight, and usually it was her that wound up apologizing.

Those days of apologizing were over, though. Seasons come and seasons go, and some should just stay gone. Still, she softened as she pictured Paul handing her the keys to the camper, saying he'd get on all right with Bill Williams until he could buy another truck. Seeing his eyes fish for a spot to rest short of her own. She'd thought on that scene too many times. Leaving without rancor is the most final of good-byes. "Stop it, girl," she said to herself. "Just stop it." She wished for a radio.

And just as she did, she heard the be-bop sound of guitar coming from the Garver rows, Wright Garver all crazy after a guy from Oklahoma named Charlie Christian, who played a new kind of jazz twenty years ago, start of the forties, and now a man named Barney Kessel, only white man in a band amongst the coloreds. Dacey Ann knew this from the confabs she heard between Wright and her husband when they hovered over guitars trying their sounds.

Paul. She missed him, but between his sometimes drinking and his rectitude when he wasn't, the worst evil of which she couldn't decide, she'd for now choose the simple, straightforward pleasure of picking single at the top of the world.

Late in the afternoon LuEthel stopped by at the base of Dacey's tree. "Turner says to fill 'em up."

"I'm about done with fightin' these lacey trees anyhow. My back muscles are saying thank you, ma'am, for the rest a-comin'. Are we gettin' old, LuEthel?"

"I get younger every evenin', Dacey Ann. The Lord and Corliss see to that." When she smiled, a dimple formed that gave her a beauty otherwise ignored.

As Dacey brought her load down, she looked at LuEthel's worn and dusty face and said, "You love that man, don't you?"

"Now, that's a fact."

"Didn't he used to whop you once in a while?"

"The meaner they act, the scareder they are, is all." The look Dacey gave her made a statement in itself. "Well, what about Paul? Cain't he sometimes be a pistol?"

"Yeah, he can. But it has to do with his bullheadedness and too many brewskis. He'd sooner punch himself in the eye than turn a hand to me."

"Then you're a lucky woman, Dacey Ann," LuEthel said. "Where's he at, by the way?"

"Over to Cove, Oregon, is where he was headed. Split up, we might do better for now, we figger."

"Oh. Uh-huh," LuEthel said.

Dacey Ann didn't much care if LuEthel believed her or not. This conversation was no more than one you might have with a stranger on a bus bench.

She poured the last of her fruit in the boxes and slipped work tickets down the side of each one. LuEthel said, "Whyn't you stop by for supper? We're just over by the Texaco. Mama's got beans, biscuits, and Spam fritters. We figure on eatin' first, then goin' to hear music at Lovey's. Early, startin' around seven. Wright and Herschel might jam."

"We'll see about that, then," Dacey said, not knowing why she said the 'we' part. She could go. Why not? She was, for all intents and purposes, a free woman again.

"Where you thinkin' of headin' after this? I mean, Turner's good for only about a week, don't you think?"

Dacey took a few seconds to answer. "I'm thinking of joining one of them commune thingies, maybe over by Petaluma, in there."

The two women were up to Dacey's truck now, and Dacey Ann was still admiring of how Paul had put together the camper on it, put it on there for her even after he knew they were splitting up. It needed a quart more color, or a big decal, but it looked bright and apple green for now, and Dacey Ann found herself running her hand over paint and plywood as if she'd never seen it before.

LuEthel said, "Oh, now, honey, you don't want

to mess with any of that hippie fallout from Frisco. They act like fools on fire sometimes."

"Could be said of all of us, I swan."

"Yeah, but."

"Yeah, but what?"

"At least this," LuEthel said. "Pickers is all kind o' people, but every one down to the bone knows if you want the fruit you got to climb the tree, and them hippies, well. Corliss is always sayin' what we need is off the gold standard and onto the soul standard. Now, hippies, they got the right idea about off the gold standard, but the rest is near to devilish." LuEthel's face was serious kin to a recent widow, kind of lost and fearful all at once.

"Pickers is all kind o' people, all right," Dacey said. "Boozers and abandoners and baby killers. Thieves and snakes and billy goats. And a few good folks like y'all. I expect the same kind of slumgullion in a commune, only maybe less."

LuEthel looked thoughtful, then said, "I guess I'd just be skittish some at leaving what I know for what I don't, come down to it."

Dacey Ann saw her own reflection in the side window of her truck and hoped her steadfast jaw would never get softened by something as cruel as fear.

She unlocked her door and got in to drive over to Turner and collect for the day, and told

LuEthel to get some rest on them bones, because she expected to see her out dancing with Corliss later.

There was a restaurant in town called Freddie's, where murals of flowering cacti extended even into the rest rooms and where Dacey knew she could cool off and sponge-bathe in the sink there, then sit at the counter and eat on her own without the Garver boys looking her over, making their silent judgments.

But when she arrived, Freddie, a big, kind-hearted woman who had worked side by side with her mother in the groves in South Carolina, would hear of nothing but letting Dacey Ann into her trailer for a real shower and a nap. She could even use the phone if she needed. "No one I know needs callin'," Dacey said, but took Freddie up on everything else.

Later, during dinner, Freddie said, "I miss your mother every *now* and then." She filled Dacey's glass with what she called her proud concoction.

Dacey Ann said, "I miss her every day."

"Well, of course you do."

Freddie leaned closer, her bosom folding onto the counter and her hand moving the glass she had just poured nearer to Dacey. "Give a taste."

Dacey Ann saw the mint leaf floating on top

and recalled the times her mother, Betty, had furnished iced tea with a mint leaf rocking on the ice.

Freddie waited for the look of approval. "Guess."

"Tastes differnt."

"Coffee, Co'Cola, lemon, and mint. What should I call it? I know. I could call it after your mother, eh? Betty's Brew. She's the one give it to me."

"My mother made this?"

"That last year before Bitsy . . . before Bitsy died. Your mother made it up foolin' around in my kitchen. I just plumb forgot about it till a coupla months ago. Then I been servin' it ever since—my proud concoction. PC for short."

"It's good."

"Your mom couldn't turn nothin' to nothin' but good. You look so much like her, you know? You don't remember that year when you and Betty and Bitsy stopped by for about a week? You don't remember that?"

Dacey shifted on her stool and looked out the window. "I remember."

"That Bitsy. She was a precious little thing," Freddie said, opening the coffeemaker and taking out the grounds, wiping the drips up with a rag. "She woulda looked like you and your mama, too. You were what, about thirteen . . . ?"

"Twelve."

"Your mama went to some kind of pieces after that, didn't she?"

"She had a problem," Dacey said in a voice that barely carried above the noise from a playing radio, a motorcycle idling at the light outside, and the old cook in the back banging pots.

"What was it, now?" Freddie asked, "I forget. Cancer of the . . . ?"

"Pancreas."

"That's just a real damn shame. Now, is that the cancer comes from too much drinking? I seem to remember that it is. I seem to remember it's a hard way to go, yes. Is that right?"

Dacey Ann didn't know whether to start hating the woman or be grateful somebody still cared. Either way, it was time to finish up and get out of there and on to whatever would come next.

Freddie said, "You know what? I kept some of your mama's letters. Uh-huh. She wrote me from Bakersfield after, you know, that thing with Bitsy. About a year, I think it was. She was asking after a job, but Martin and me, we could hardly keep the place open as it was. I still, matter of fact, close this place up at eight. Anyway, I kept them letters because she wrote so nice, you know? Just the other day I come across 'em. I was going to pitch 'em but must have been somethin' in the air made me not, 'cause here you are. If you'll be at Lovey's tonight, so will I. There's only a few—"

"I'm plannin' on it." Dacey Ann was standing to reach for the money in her jeans when the door opened and let in a reminder of the day's heat.

Freddie seemed to gain relief from sorry thoughts by the interruption. She sent a greeting to the two men in cowboy hats and denim who spoke her name louder than was needed while they gave Dacey Ann a glance. Dacey left money on the counter and took her leave, saying thanks and meaning it.

Letters from her mama, Dacey Ann thought as she stepped outside. Dacey Ann had almost nothing left from her mother. Her mother's writing, what did it look like? She could hardly remember.

She looked across the road at Bilbee's Country Store near where she was parked and saw Turner's truck with both doors open. The two Mexican workers were sitting there, drinking pop from bottles and eating hardboiled eggs.

Before she reached the sidewalk, Turner stepped out of the store. He glanced at her, then the nationals, and said, "I'm gonna let those two go."

"Bum workers?"

"They could drown in their own sweat, but that ain't the point."

"Well, thanks for looking out for us, Turner."

He nodded toward the pair and said, "That's dinner, them eggs and soda. They send the rest home across the border, I guess. Well, you goin' to Lovey's or what?" He eyed the flower-print dress Dacey Ann had on.

"Thinkin' about it."

"See you bright and early."

"That you will. G'night, Turner."

He touched his finger to his straw hat and went on his way toward the hardware store.

Dacey Ann took a few steps, then turned back to the truck. She was up close before the nearest national understood she had come to gain his attention. "Here," she said, and handed him two folded five-dollar bills. The man looked at them, then shook his head no and tried to hand the money back but Dacey flagged her hand at him, smiled, and crossed the street after a car full of teenagers hanging out the window and yelling at Lord knows what.

It was near eight already, and Dacey Ann was the kind of lonesome could get a girl in trouble. But she guessed she'd go on over to hear the Garver boys jam if they were going to. She wouldn't have to give them all her company. There'd be other boys to dance with, should that come to pass.

And coming off Freddie so soon and all that talk of things, Dacey Ann saw her mother on *her* way to a place like Lovey's, in Springfield, Oregon, only it wasn't to have a good time, it was to find that no-account husband and drag him home. The memory increased as she walked, and she saw them fighting again that night, only all she'd really done was hear them because Dacey Ann had hidden her head beneath the pillow. Bitsy, she slipped *under* the bed, as she often did to keep out of the way or to lessen the fearfulness outside from a thunderstorm or inside from a human one.

Sometime in the night, or the wee hours, or the early later morning, Dacey Ann heard a scream. A blood-curdling scream, as the books say. It was her mother's tone, gargled and strangled and graveled, but she knew it from all other possible sounds, and the terror it evoked was a rod of white-hot iron driven through Dacey's own trillion melting cells.

For Bitsy had not hidden under the bed. Barbara "Bitsy" Lee Little, six years old, died of injuries, the newspaper said, when her father attempted to move a tractor from the side of the house. The child was asleep on the ground. Bitsy could just sleep anywhere. Maybe it was under a tractor or under a bed or beside a hay bale or even in a cupboard, where she hid one time playing hide-and-seek.

Bitsy'd be eighteen now. She'd be going to Lovey's with Dacey Ann, likely. They'd be barelegged and sassy, the two of them, looking good in their clothes, making eyes and half-promises, dreaming of futures better than what they'd likely get.

Ernest Little coming to Stockton? Forget it. He sure as hell didn't belong in the orchard next to her elbow, souring the air she breathed.

Vernon Garver was the one sent Dacey Ann a drink. She was finding her way to a table when the bar girl took a beer off a tray loaded with others and put it in Dacey's hand while she was passing by. "The guy with the goatee and black CAT Diesel cap at the bar," said the woman.

Dacey threaded back over and said thanks. "Where's ever'body?"

"Up there," Vernon answered, nodding clear across the room with the big dance floor and up to the stage, where the band was having at a country song. They all looked different with cowboy hats on. There was Herschel with his patch, sprinkled with red sequins. There was Wright, heavy of hat and square of jaw. There were guys she didn't know . . . and, damn!, there was . . .

"Ernest is sure 'nough hootin' on that acoustic," Vernon said.

Dacey Ann switched away from the view and said, "I'd as leave you didn't mention that man's name so soon after supper."

"Wowzie. LuEthel is right. You can be hard as a shell."

"There's things you know and things you don't know, Vernon." She'd give him credit, Vernon. At least he didn't argue.

Ernest Eugene's story was that he and his wife had been drinking and fighting, yes, and it was his way to up and leave no matter there was food in the cupboard or hearts crying for love. When his wife hid the keys to the car this time to keep him from going, he grabbed up the tractor key over the sink on the back porch, thinking he'd white-line old John Deere out of that sorry place forever. Only he never got five yards.

Next day the newspaper said officers had to subdue him and charged him with reckless intoxication and assault on a peace officer, which turned into involuntary manslaughter on Bitsy's behalf and put him in county for eighteen and a half months. That's what Vernon should know. That's a baby-killing, slinking scoundrel for ya, you want to see one.

Dacey Ann recalled Paul saying the man still

had some good in him. But Ernest Eugene had gone up river more than once after that. Ta-kill-ya, as her dad called it, put him there. He'd down a water glass half full of tequila and reach for the bottle again before a swatter could connect to a fly.

"You got more kin comin'," Vernon said, "what I understand."

"Huh? Who? Who's comin'?"

"Paul. Him and Eugene met up in Marysville."

"I sure wish people would stop following me all over creation."

In spite of herself, a warm rush flooded her parts. Her eyes searched the crowd for that tall guy whose easy walk and curling smile had first set her skin afire. But wherever he was, he wasn't here.

And her eyes sought out that weasel of a man people called her father. Sought him out with contempt and a rise of memory wrapped in a kind of hopeful expectation that only increased her anger. When her gaze did light upon him, she almost didn't recognize him. He was white-headed and much smaller than she remembered, and he was sitting at a table with LuEthel Garver and Minnie Jean. Good. Maybe holy folks would light up his decrepit soul.

"Vernon," Dacey Ann said, "let's dance."

*   *   *

In a while Dacey Ann made her way to the ladies' room. Ernest Eugene still hadn't seen her, but she didn't care if he did.

There was a line waiting. Minnie Jean was at the sink, wetting a paper towel and tapping off sweat on the top of her bosom. Minnie Jean could dance, for a religious woman. "Life ain't all about cherry pickin', is it, Dacey Ann?" she said, blooming the apples of her cheeks. "Say, I was talking to your dad. You gonna go say hello?"

"He ain't going to play, is he?" Dacey Ann was thinking she might listen, but she sure wouldn't dance to that man's pickin'.

"I think he'll be around awhile. I think he's going to be getting up there." Her hair had sprung free from the knot in back and showed around her face like a silver-sprayed wreath. In a softer voice she said, "Step on out here a minute, if you please. The line will let you butt back in, won't you, ladies?"

Minnie Jean stood at the open door with Dacey where they could see the stage and let the music in. Minnie Jean said, "Honey, before we die, every one of us needs to know what we're running from. I advise you listen to your heart." Her eyes shifted to where her son Herschel and Ernest Eugene Little were fighting each other onstage for who would get to wear the sequined eyepatch, stretching the band so the one loop snapped off, then knocking each other for it. "That there's a man you'd do good getting to know. Now, go make your bladder gladder. I'm gonna go fiddle the bugs off a sweet potato vine," she said, and headed stage-wise herself.

Dacey Ann listened, watched Minnie Jean and Ernest Eugene and the rest of the motley Garver clan do their thing with the other band boys, and then she decided morning came early and stepped out onto the sidewalk to get to her truck. There was Freddie Elkins getting out of her old Studebaker after finding the only space right in front of the club.

"Leavin' already? Here you go, gal," she said, and handed Dacey Ann a lunch sack of letters. "Blessings on ya." Freddie heaved herself up on the rise of the sidewalk and then the next step leading into the club, and Dacey Ann found herself once again saying thanks while the older woman vanished inside.

By dim light, with just a sheet over her legs, Dacey Ann read those letters in her camper, while off on the highway she heard the whine of big rigs coursing by. She read the letters, as her father used to say, till the cows came home. Then she read them again and then again—because buried in the mundane details of a woman's reported life was a soul's plight worse than any Dacey Ann could have imagined.

What hour she went to sleep she didn't know. The next day she was banging at Freddie's door at noontime. It was a Sunday, and she had to wait till then because Turner did have work for her, but being in those trees was almost a pain she couldn't bear, her anxiousness so great to hear from Freddie's own mouth what the letters seemed to say.

And Freddie confirmed it. Sat her down in the kitchen with the oilcloth spread over the table and a tiny vase of daisies set in the middle and her proud concoction minus the mint slid in front of Dacey and said, "Your daddy didn't take them tractor keys, baby. Your mommy did. It was her was gonna take the car, so Ernest wouldn't be leaving."

"But that can't be," Dacey Ann said, not willing to believe.

"She was drinking way hard, probably tryin' to outdrink the man she hated and loved all of a piece. Ernest snatched the keys away from her. So she went and grabbed up the tractor keys. It was your mama drove that tractor over her baby, honey, and your daddy tooked the blame. And that is what brought her to the slippery slope. I'm not all that happy to be the one to tell you, but you're old enough to know it now and get on with your life."

Dacey Ann pinned her gaze on Freddie with all kinds of interpretations going on in her mind. She argued with Freddie twenty minutes on every one. But at the end, it was no good going back to the orchard on this day. Dacey Ann left Freddie's small, white-painted house, purged of all feeling, good or bad, and walked out into a dry heat hot enough to clean meat from bones.

She sat in her truck with the back of the seat searing the bare spots on her calves, her thighs, her elbows and the scoop down her back. She glanced just once in the mirror and saw a fool looking back.

Then she turned the key in the ignition and rolled down the road toward Turner land, with an unfamiliar quiet in her veins and an eye out for anything looked like a Little. She'd tell him ladder work cleared her vision. Say she was sorry it took so long. She'd ask if he'd ever had cherry soup—sort of a new flavor of beans. And if she was lucky, she'd crank a smile out of that guitar-lickin' man.

Noreen Ayres

AFTERWORD

The impulse for "Ladder Work" may have come from half-remembered experiences I had as a child when I lived in Oregon and picked cherries and loganberries . . . somewhere, on someone's farm. I may have picked only one day or one week, I don't remember. Doubtless, the *amount* I picked would not have aptly fed a raccoon, but what I carried away were memories of vibrant life: smells, colors, shapes, the antics of worms, beetles, birds, and critters.

My first published short story, "The Tomato Farm," was born in the dry flats of Lodi, California, where my parents sharecropped the year I was six. I lived five more years on a farm in Oregon. More recently, I've been in the fields in California as part of charity work, harvesting beans, cabbage, corn, and potatoes, dragging gunny sacks through muddy rows, leaving shoes stuck in the muck, getting covered with itchy corn sheddings, thinking I might faint from the heat but not wanting to stop until I got just that one last bunch . . . over there. I loved it—but then, I didn't have to make a living stooped, dry, and dirty. But I will say this: there's something about plodding in the furrows that gives you back to life, connects you to the flow of time and the fundamentals, puts a cocky human in her place.

The people in this story represent the ones I like to write about most: hardworking. Full of foolish (perhaps) hopes. On the fringe but owning frames of morality. The ones with wind at their backs, restless. They fall. They rise. They keep on keeping on, as the saying goes. Ladder work—one rung at a time. It's in all our lives. It just goes by different names.

A Stillness at the Heart

Diana Gabaldon with her parents and baby sister, Theresa, on the day of Theresa's baptism.

FOREWORD

When I sold my first book, I called my father to tell him about it. He was both amazed (I hadn't told him I was *writing* a book) and thrilled, and told me with a lump in the throat how proud he was of me, what a wonderful thing it was, how pleased my mother (who died when I was nineteen) would have been. We finished this touching conversation and hung up. A moment later the phone rang; it was my father, who, without pausing to say hello, blurted out, "Don't quit your job!"

The youngest of fifteen children born to a New Mexican farming family, my father never knew his own father—who died when he was three months old—but did know a lot about economics and the value of an education. He worked from the time he was five, cutting wild asparagus from the roadsides and selling bunches door to door with the goat cheeses his mother made. When they moved to Los Angeles some years later, he sold papers; one of the high points of his early life was that he had sold a paper every day to John Wayne, who lived in a hotel nearby at the time.

At thirteen he moved to Flagstaff, Arizona, and went to work in an elder brother's restaurant as a dishwasher. By eighteen he was a fully qualified professional chef—managing in the meantime not only to graduate from high school, but to become a multi-sport athlete, an All-State quarterback, and to be inducted into the high school's Hall of Fame.

He got married, got a college degree and a teaching certificate, had two daughters, and embarked on a career that spanned teaching, school administration, state, regional, and national politics—and through it all he continued to cook, at nights and on weekends to help support his young family, then catering dinners for six hundred or so at a time in order to raise money for his political campaigns, or to benefit whatever charitable cause had asked him to donate his skills.

There were hundreds of news photos, snapshots, and professional portraits of him, but when I went through his desk after his death, I found one clipping, showing him in apron and padded mitts, grinning as he pulled a tray of enchiladas from the oven. Over it was written the only opinion I ever saw him express of a likeness of himself—"Good photo!" it said.

Of the fifteen children, he was the only one with a college education—and he knew the value of it.

"Anyone can make money if they're willing to work hard," he told my sister and me. "But you need an education to know how to live well." Consequently, he prodded us to go as far as possible in the direction of scholarship.

"You're such a poor judge of character," he'd say to me, "you're sure to marry some bum. Be sure to get a good education, so you can support your family!"

(Now, as a matter of fact, I *didn't* marry a bum—I married a wonderful man twenty-one years ago, and still have him, thank you—but I did get a Ph.D. in ecology, and a master's degree in marine biology. My sister is a professor of law.)

At the same time, I remember one other thing my father said: "Money is only important if you don't have any. Family is the only thing that's *always* important."

He was right.

A STILLNESS AT THE HEART

I was still working that Friday night, though getting ready to shut things down since it was after three a.m. When the phone rang, I looked at the caller ID and saw my father-in-law's number come up. My father-in-law Max is eighty-one, my mother-in-law eighty-five, and both in fairly feeble health, so I was already mentally preparing to rouse Doug, dress, and go out to meet the emergency when I picked up the phone.

It was Max himself, though; he said that my stepmother's sister had just called him, being unable to reach me (in the stress of the moment, they must have been calling my old phone number)—my dad was at Good Samaritan trauma center, and that was all he knew.

I woke Doug—scaring him out of a sound sleep—got dressed, thinking as I did so that I must take a warm sweatshirt, because hospital waiting rooms are always cold, and no telling how long I might be there. I left Doug with the kids, promising to call as soon as I found out anything, promised not to drive too fast, repelled the efforts of the dog who wanted to go with me—I didn't know how long he might be left in the car alone—and left.

I was driving carefully, all right, but in that state of nervous agitation attendant on being pulled out of the solitude of the night to face unknown anxieties. I was praying, of course, in the unformed fashion one does when in the face of such things. And then, some distance down the highway, that stopped.

The praying stopped, the agitation stopped, the anxiety disappeared. It was 3:26 by the dashboard clock, which is always two minutes slow. I haven't seen the death certificate, but I don't need to.

Everything was simply . . . still.

I was still driving; a car passed me now and then. The lights went by, I took note of the road signs, but my heartbeat and my breathing had gone back to that state of quiet solitude from which I'd come. I tried to form a prayer, but the words wouldn't come. Not that I couldn't think of them, but that there was no need; whatever I would have asked had already been answered.

Everything was just . . . peaceful.

I sometimes feel my mother near me, sometimes summoned, sometimes not. She isn't always there when I call, but always comes again, sometime. I reached for her, in the middle of the stillness, and felt her there, but it wasn't she who answered me.

I daresay I haven't thought of my grandmother Inez once in ten years, if that. She was very old when I was born, died when I was eleven (I remember only because she died on my birthday). We saw her once a year, pro forma: a tiny old lady who smelled funny and spoke no English; we learned a few Spanish phrases which we repeated to her like Latin prayers in church; understood, but with little sense of communication.

She came into my mind then, though. White-haired still, but with her face quite young—and with what appeared to be her own teeth rather than her dentures, I noticed.

"*Somos duras,*" she said to me, and then, "*Somos.*"

Dura is a word that means "hard." Depending on the usage, it means everything from difficult or painful (things are hard) to tough and resilient—strong. *Somos* means "We are."

"Okay," I said.

I reached the hospital and parked in the visitors lot. There was no need for hurry, and I didn't want to take a space that might be needed near the emergency entrance. It was a gentle night, very balmy. I passed a woman sitting on a bench outside the outpatient surgery department, smoking. I smiled at her and nodded as I passed.

I walked up the long ramp to the emergency

trauma center; it's on the second floor. Two of my stepmother's sisters were standing outside, crouched over their cellular phones like Secret Service agents. I touched one on the shoulder and she turned; her face crumpled up with grief, and she embraced me, squeezing hard and thumping my back.

"It's okay," I said, after a little of this. "I'm all right."

"*I'm* not!" she said, and clung to me, sobbing, as we went in.

"*Somos duras*," said my grandmother again.

I saw his feet first. They're just like mine, short and wide, remarkably small in proportion to his body. I don't have sparse black hairs on my toes, and he had a chronic nail condition that made his toenails thick and yellow. The same round heel, though, and short, high arch, the broad, short toes that point up just a little when the foot is at rest—ugly feet, but happy feet.

There were several people around him; he was lying on a gurney, half covered by a flannel sheet. My stepmother was there, holding his hand; I took no notice of the others. I needed to see his face.

He looked as he always did when asleep; he had a habit of falling asleep watching television. In the years after my mother died, before he married again, I would always get up at midnight when I was in the house with him to wake him and tell him to go to bed. I think he was afraid to go to bed alone.

His ears were faintly purple. My son has his ears; a smooth clamshell with a fleshy lobe. There was a deep crease across each lobe; I'd read somewhere that that's an indication of a predisposition to heart disease.

I had thought I would be seized by grief at sight of him, and was surprised to feel instead the most peculiar sense of . . . completion. He was a happy man, for the most part, but not in any way a peaceful one; he had jagged edges that crossed his personality like fissures through a glacier. Always restless, always moving. A vicious and accomplished hater, a bearer of implacable grudges. Now that was finished. Not gone, exactly, but *finished*. Now he had a peace that he had always missed; he was complete.

"*Somos*," said my grandmother very softly, and I knew what she meant.

My stepmother embraced me, and I her.

"What happened?" I said.

She said she'd gone to bed at midnight; Dad followed her a little later. She woke about a quarter to three, because his breathing had changed; he was snoring very heavily. She poked him to roll over, and it changed again, to "horrible noises." She turned on the light, saw his face, and knew something was wrong; ran to the front bedroom to get her sister and brother-in-law, who were visiting from California.

They ran back and did CPR while my stepmother called 911. They live only a few blocks from a major hospital, so the paramedics arrived in two minutes. They worked on him there and, on the way to the hospital, managed to (she said) restart "part of his heart muscle" but could not revive him.

An unknown man at my father's head came to shake hands with my stepmother, explaining that my father had been "nice and warm" when he arrived; everything was all right. The priest, come to give the last anointing; there is a popular supposition that if the body is at least warm, the soul is still close enough to benefit.

He was still warm; everyone had a hand on his body—bare shoulder, hand, or the huge, round mound of his stomach—he was always overweight, but carried it all there. I laid a hand on him, too, for a minute. Then looked up and realized that I was looking at my uncle Albert, who lives in Albuquerque: my father's last surviving brother, also my godfather. I hadn't noticed him at first, because he looks like my father—all the brothers had a strong facial resemblance. It seemed completely unremarkable to see my father lying down and standing up simultaneously.

Under the rather surreal circumstances, it at first seemed quite natural for Albert to be there. It's a very large family, and all through my youth, whenever someone died, all the relatives would gather, going from Albuquerque to California or back the other way; they'd all stay briefly at our house, as Flagstaff is midway. Then it dawned on me that my father had been dead for less than half an hour; I knew it takes at least an hour to fly from Albuquerque.

"What are you doing here?" I blurted, thinking a bit too late that I hoped this sounded only astonished, and not ungracious.

He was solemn, but not outwardly upset. He's the last of the brothers, and in his seventies; he's seen a lot of death.

"I was here," he said, with a little shrug. He'd come, by coincidence—or not—for a New Year's visit. He and Dad had stayed up all evening, talking and laughing, then went to bed at twelve-thirty.

My stepmother's sisters—three of them by then—came and went, bringing Kleenex, cups of water. The hospital attendant came now and then, a quiet, compassionate young woman, bearing forms to be signed, questions to be answered.

Which mortuary? Burial or cremation? And—she apologized, saying by law she had to ask us—would we consider organ donation?

Yes, I said firmly, hands on my father's stomach. I felt strongly about it; I could feel my stepmother hesitate. She is the kindest and gentlest of people—no one else could have stayed married to my father—but consequently she can be bullied. I would have done it if I had to, but she said yes.

"But are they usable?" I asked, glancing down at him. "He's sixty-seven."

"I don't know," the young woman said, frowning uncertainly. "I'll check." She did. The corneas, she said; they could use the eyes and corneas.

The sisters touched him constantly, exclaiming every so often, "He's still warm here!" and clutching whichever part it was (my father's often expressed opinion to my stepmother—frequently given in their hearing—was, "Your sisters are very good people, *but* . . .").

I stood aside a little. They asked if I wanted to be alone with him for a little while, and I said no. It wasn't necessary. It wasn't necessary to touch the body again; I had no feeling that this was my father. I knew exactly where he was; he was with me, with his wives, with his brother, with his mother. *Somos.* We are.

I was not upset at all, though I wept now and then in sheer emotional reaction. After a time it became clear that there was nothing more to do—and yet it seemed impossible to leave. Albert said quietly that he would go back to the house to rest. More of my stepmother's family came—she has a huge family, all very loyal and supportive.

I looked very carefully. What of his features remained in me and my children, that I could still see—what was unique, that I must remember now, because I would never see again? My hands are his, as well as the feet; my sister has his eyes. The swell of broad shoulders I've seen in my son since his birth; my youngest daughter shares the shape of his calves.

At last the young woman came back and said softly but firmly that she would need to take him now, "to finish taking care of him." I touched one foot, said, "Good-bye, Dad," and walked out without looking back.

Out in the waiting room, we met a young man from the organ-donor program, and went with him to fill out the necessary forms. I have had fewer experiences more surreal than sitting in a consultation room at five o'clock in the morning answering questions as to whether my father had ever accepted money or drugs for sex, or had sex with another man.

The answers (no, by the way—or at least not so far as *I* know) all proving satisfactory, we left at last. I prevented any of the sisters coming with me with some difficulty, and headed home across the dark city. It seemed important to get home before the night ended, maybe because I thought it might seem more real by daylight.

So now there are rips and rawnesses, surges of grief that catch at throat and belly. All the difficulties and distractions of dealing with sudden death.

And yet I remember, and reach to touch that great stillness, like a smooth stone in my pocket.

Somos.

I was . . . astonished.

About the Authors

NOREEN AYRES

Noreen Ayres is the author of two crime novels, *A World the Color of Salt* and *Carcass Trade* (Morrow/Avon), featuring civilian crime-lab worker Smokey Brandon, ex-cop, ex-stripper; and of *Sorting Out Darkness,* a poetry collection. Her short story "Delta Double-Deal" appears in the Mystery Writers of America anthology for 1999.

Raised in California, Oklahoma, and Oregon, Noreen has worked in the construction, engineering, computer, aerospace, and petroleum industries as a technical publications writer and manager. She is a competition handgun shooter and ballroom dancer, currently residing in Texas, with her husband, father, and dog "Bubba."

CAROLE NELSON DOUGLAS

Former award-winning journalist Carole Nelson Douglas is a multigenre author of thirty-five novels. *Good Night, Mr. Holmes* initiated four historical mysteries about the only woman to outwit Sherlock Holmes, American diva Irene Adler. It was a *New York Times* Notable Book and won American Mystery and *Romantic Times* awards. Douglas's contemporary mystery series features a hard-boiled feline P.I., Midnight Louie (Sam Spade with hairballs), whose first-purrson feline narrations in short fiction and novels (*Cat in a Crimson Haze, Cat in a Diamond Dazzle,* etc.), have won awards from the Cat Writers' Association and *Mostly Murder* magazine.

Douglas has always loved cats, writing, and water, moving from landlocked Minnesota to the Gulf state of Texas to write fiction full-time in 1984. She and her husband, Sam Douglas, an artist-craftsman, collect strays: seven cats and a dog, and have a vintage clothing collection that began with unclaimed items from her grandparents' house.

EILEEN DREYER

Award-winning, bestselling author Eileen Dreyer, known as Kathleen Korbel to her Silhouette romance readers, has published twenty romance novels and five suspense novels under her own name for HarperCollins, including

Brain Dead, Nothing Personal, Bad Medicine, and *A Man to Die For*, all medical thrillers, which should come as no surprise, considering her background.

A native of St. Louis, where she still lives with her husband, Rick, and two children, Dreyer spent twenty years walking hospital halls, sixteen of those as a trauma nurse. She now writes full-time, at least when she's not spending darn near every holiday and yearly vacations with her six siblings, various in-laws and offspring, and her father, who is, indeed, a CPA—and darned proud of it.

DIANA GABALDON

Diana Gabaldon is the author of the award-winning *Outlander* series, which began in 1991 with the time-travel classic *Outlander*, continued through *Dragonfly in Amber* and *Voyager*, and most recently, the *New York Times* bestseller *Drums of Autumn*. The internationally bestselling series chronicles the adventures of twentieth-century nurse/physician Claire Randall, and her eighteenth-century Highland lover, Jamie Fraser. There are two further novels planned in the series, plus a prequel volume, and *The Outlandish Companion*, which will be released in summer of

1999. In addition, Ms. Gabaldon is working on a contemporary mystery series set in Phoenix.

Dr. Gabaldon holds graduate degrees in science (M.S., marine biology, Scripps Institute of Oceanography; Ph.D., behavioral ecology, Northern Arizona University), and spent a dozen years as a university professor with an expertise in scientific computation before beginning to write fiction. She has written scientific articles and textbooks, worked as an editor on the Macmillan *Encyclopedia of Computers*, founded the scientific-computation journal *Scientific Software Quarterly*, and has written numerous comic-book scripts for Walt Disney. She presently lives in Scottsdale, Arizona, with her husband, three children, and a large number of animals (both wild and domestic, though the animals are not inclined to observe the distinction).

EILEEN GOUDGE

Over the past twelve years, Eileen Goudge has published five novels with Viking, *Garden of Lies*, *Such Devoted Sisters*, *Blessing in Disguise*, *Trail of Secrets*, and *Thorns of Truth*. All titles are available, both in paperback (Signet) and in audio, and have been translated into twenty-five languages as well. A former welfare mother who wrote her way out of poverty, Eileen has been featured in major newspapers and magazines, and makes regular TV appearances.

Eileen is married to broadcaster Sandy Kenyon, formerly of CNN and currently with WINS. They met on the radio, fell in love over the phone, and in 1996 were wed. They now live in an 1850's carriage house in New York City. Eileen has two grown children from a former marriage, Michael and Mary. "In real life, there are no such things as happy endings," she says, "only happy beginnings." Eileen is the second of six children. Her father, Robert James Goudge, recently passed away.

J. A. JANCE

Since 1985, J. A. Jance has published over twenty books. Most fall in the police procedural category. Detective J. P. Beaumont (fourteen books in print) hails from Seattle, Washington, while Sheriff Joanna Brady (six books so far) calls southeastern Arizona home. J. A. Jance is also the author of *Hour of the Hunter*, a psychological thriller set among the Tohono O'othham of southern Arizona.

In writing her books, J. A. calls on a lifetime of varied experiences, which include stints of seven years spent teaching and ten in life insurance sales. As bi-regional as her characters, J. A. has divided her life between Arizona and Washington state. She has a husband, five children, three grandchildren, and three dogs.

FAYE KELLERMAN

Faye Kellerman is the author of a dozen books including the *New York Times* bestselling Peter Decker/Rina Lazarus series. The first novel in the series, *Ritual Bath,* won the Macavity award for best novel. Faye Kellerman's novels combine gritty police procedurals with an in-depth look into the world of Orthodox Judaism.

Kellerman's father, Oscar Marder Teitelbaum Marder, was born in Kovel, Poland, around the Jewish New Year in 1921 and was arbitrarily given the birth date of September twenty-fifth. The family emigrated to America six years later, settling in St. Louis, Missouri, because an uncle lived there and signed for them. In his forties, he changed his name from Oscar Teitelbaum to Oscar Marder—his mother's maiden name—not for PC reasons, but because Marder was easier to spell and pronounce. He died in November 1974. Kellerman has trouble remembering the exact date. She has blocked it from memory.

JILL MORGAN

Jill Morgan is the author of sixteen novels in the genres of suspense, ecological thrillers, horror, fantasy, and historical. She was forty years old before she sold her first novel, *Emerald Destiny*, a historical saga set in Ireland. Over the next ten years she sold fifteen more novels in rapid succession. When not writing as Jill Morgan, some of her books have been published under the pseudonyms of Meg Griffin, Jessica Pierce, Morgan Fields, and Meredith Morgan, as well as J. M. Morgan. Six of her novels are for teen and younger readers. Her short fiction has been published in numerous anthologies. She has coedited six anthologies, including *Great Writers & Kids Write Spooky Stories*, voted Best Children's Book of 1995 by *Rocky Mountain News*. Her recent anthologies include *Mothers & Daughters* and this volume, both published by Signet.

Jill Morgan was born in Texas, where many of her novels are set, but now lives in southern California with her husband, John, a high school science teacher. They are the parents of two grown sons and a daughter, who make them very proud.

BILLIE SUE MOSIMAN

Billie Sue Mosiman has published eight suspense novels since 1984. *Wireman,* her first, was recently reprinted by Leisure Books. Mosiman won an Edgar award nomination for her novel *Night Cruise* and a Stoker award nomination for *Widow.* Always active as a short story writer, Billie Sue Mosiman has had more than a hundred stories published in various magazines and anthologies.

Billie Sue celebrated her thirtieth anniversary of marriage to Lyle Mosiman in 1998. She has two daughters and five grandchildren, all of whom live in the Houston, Texas, area. Her father and mother, Leroy and Yvonne Smith, live in Livingston, Texas.

MAXINE O'CALLAGHAN

Maxine O'Callaghan's novels of mystery and dark suspense include a series that features Orange County P.I. Delilah West, credited by many critics as the first of the new female private investigators. O'Callaghan's work has been nominated for the Anthony and the Shamus awards in the mystery field, and the Bram Stoker for horror.

O'Callaghan has two grown children and a

grandson. A long-time resident of southern California, she spends a lot of time in Arizona where her daughter lives and regards Phoenix as her second home.

MARILYN REYNOLDS

Marilyn Reynolds is currently at work on a new young adult novel and a collection of personal essays. The six books in Reynolds's popular teen fiction series, *True Life from Hamilton High,* have been highly acclaimed by the American Library Association and the New York City Library, as well as by students and teachers across the country. *Detour for Emmy,* one of the novels in this series, received the 1995/96 South Carolina Young Adult Book Award. Reynolds received an Emmy nomination for her work on the *ABC Afterschool Special* adaptation of her novel *Too Soon for Jeff.* Reynolds's essays and short stories have appeared in major national newspapers, and in other anthologies and literary magazines.

After having taught high school in southern California for twenty-six years, Marilyn Reynolds now lives in the Sacramento area with her husband, Mike, where they indulge themselves in daytime movies and walks along the American River. They are the parents of three grown children, Sharon, Cindi, and Matt, and the grandparents of Ashley, Kerry, and Subei.

MARY WILLIS WALKER

Mary Willis Walker's first novel, *Zero at the Bone* (1991), won the Agatha and Macavity awards for best first mystery and was nominated for an Edgar award. *The Red Scream* (1994) won the Edgar award for best mystery/suspense novel. *Under the Beetle's Cellar* (1995) won the Hammett award from the International Association of Crime Writers for excellence in crime writing, the Macavity award from Mystery Readers International, the Anthony award from Bouchercon, and was named one of the best books of the year by *Publishers Weekly* and Mostly Murder. Her fourth novel, *All the Dead Lie Down,* was published in 1998.

Walker lives in Austin, Texas, which is the setting for all four of her books. She is working on a new book and still trying to train Daphne, her maniacal golden retriever, to have a little dignity. She enjoys spending time with her two grown daughters and her father, who at ninety plays tennis twice a day and is always game for an adventure.